Books By Joab Stieglitz

The Utgarda Series
The Old Man's Request
The Missing Medium
The Other Realm
The Hunter in the Shadows:
The Worlds I Know

How to Be an Awesome Game Master

Tales of Gods and Monsters

Larry Nodens Mysteries
Designed for Slaughter
Bound for Duty
Trials of the Overlords
Cult of Personality

Designed for Slaughter

Larry Nodens #1

Joab Stieglitz

Dedication

This book is dedicated to my wife, without whose continual support and relentless encouragement it may never have been finished.

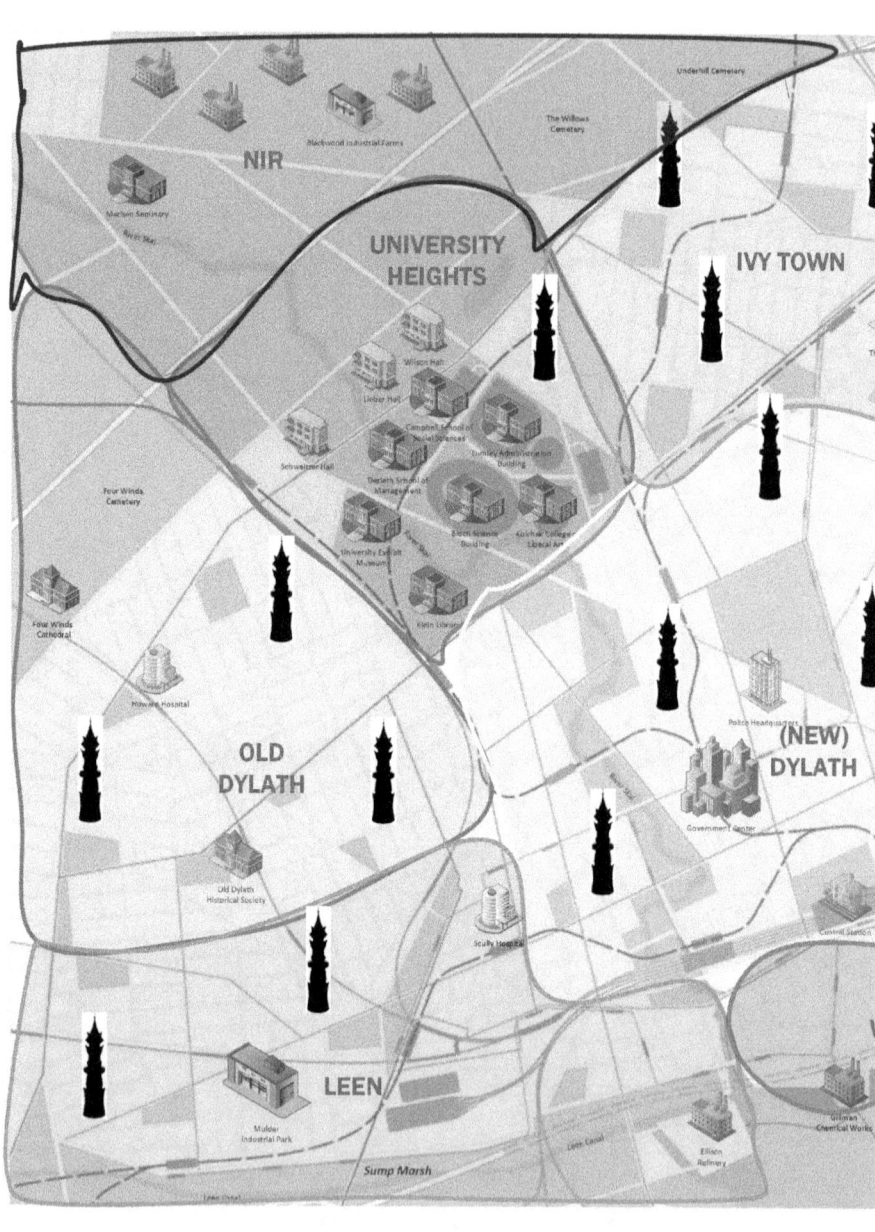

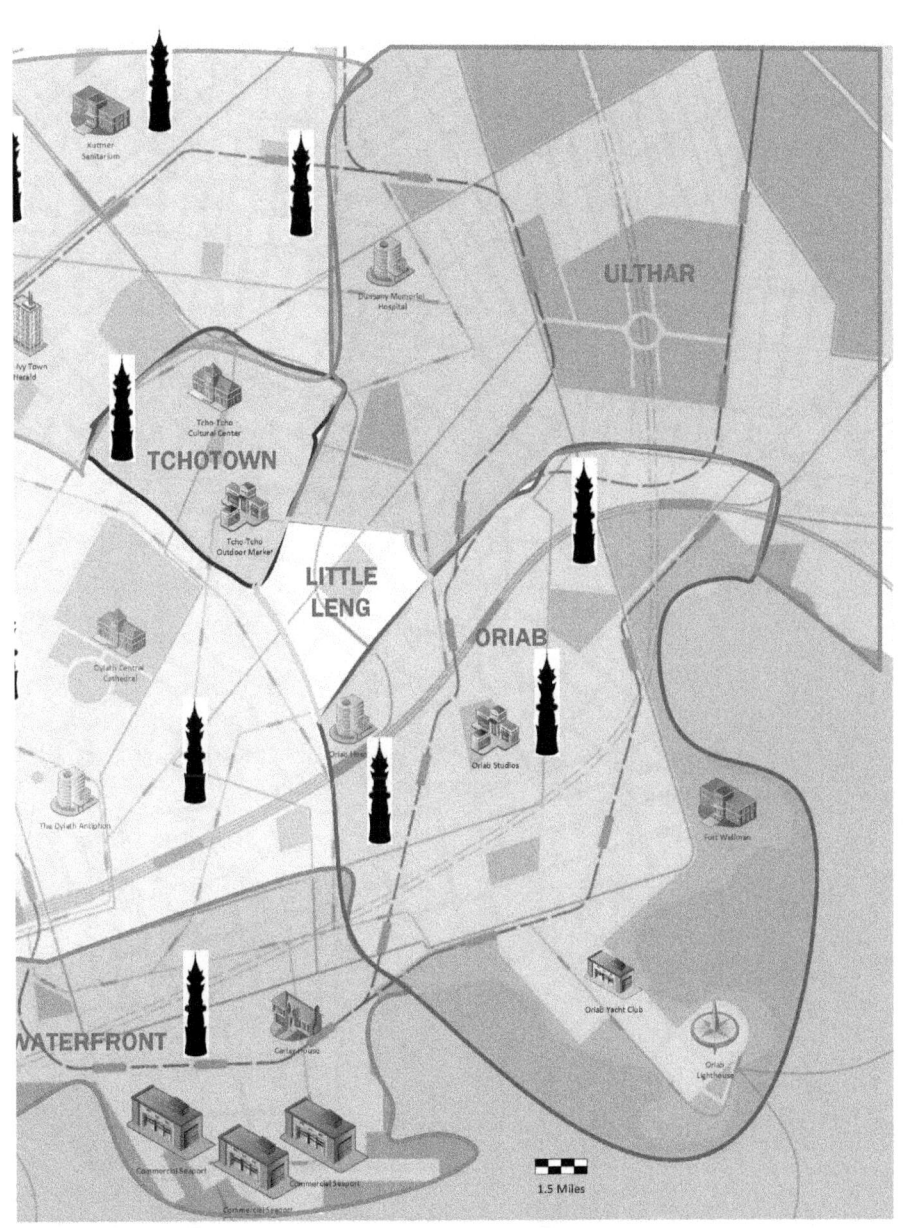

Chapter 1

Susan Jones hurriedly made her way down the dimly lit street, surrounded by ominous shadows that seemed to lurk in every corner. The sound of her black, patent leather boots echoed loudly with each brisk step she took. The street was eerily deserted and filled with an uncomfortable silence. She could no longer hear the thumping music from the club just a few blocks away, the vibrations of which had resonated through her body.

Her boots matched the ensemble she wore - a revealing transparent day-glow yellow plastic mini-dress, accessorized with a patent leather strapless bra and a thong that stood out conspicuously. Merilee had insisted that this club in Little Leng was the perfect place to be noticed, and she had been right. Susan couldn't deny that she looked hotter than her friend, especially in this outfit. However, it was Merilee who had caught the attention of the enigmatic Overlord, with his blue skin and four arms, amidst the crowd. He had swiftly maneuvered towards Merilee, disregarding Susan, and abruptly replaced her on the dance floor.

Susan was accustomed to playing second fiddle to Merilee when it came to receiving attention, but it still stung. Although she had managed to attract some admirers of her own, she knew she was always the second choice. But this time, her friend had abandoned her completely. One moment they were dancing together, and the next, Merilee and the Overlord were engaged in a passionate encounter right there on the dance floor before vanishing into thin air, transported to some unknown location.

They had taken the Underground to the Tcho-Tcho Cultural Center, following the captivating music through a maze of narrow alleys and courtyards. Susan's only guiding landmarks were the imposing black towers that had materialized all over Dylath-Leen with the arrival of the Overlords. These colossal monoliths towered above the dilapidated buildings adorned with the peculiar characters of the Lengite language.

Gazing up from street level, Susan could see the Tchotown tower piercing the dark purple sky. The stars above seemed to rearrange themselves, as they did every night, providing her with a sense of familiarity. With determination, she ascended the sloping hill towards the alien structure, aware that Ivy Town lay just a few blocks beyond it. Once she reached that brightly lit and bustling neighborhood, she would finally feel a semblance of safety, or as safe as one could be in the presence of the Overlords. However, she first had to navigate through Tchotown.

Susan froze in her tracks as she caught a scraping noise emanating from somewhere nearby. She strained her ears, listening intently for a moment, but the sound did not repeat. Hastening her pace, she attempted to drown out her thoughts with the rapid squeaking of her boots, reminiscent of the encounter with Bram in his bed the previous night. She welcomed the distraction and continued purposefully towards the black tower, turning a corner only to come face to face with horror.

A Ravager. The enormous alien predator held the lifeless body of an elderly woman in its talons, greedily devouring her entrails with multiple suckers protruding from its face. Susan's stomach churned as she witnessed this gruesome scene unfold before her. Despite the glowing radiance of her dress, the creature appeared oblivious to her presence.

Instinctively, Susan retreated into a dark alley, her trembling hand finding the small can of mace in her micropurse. In her panic, her phone slipped from her grasp, clattering loudly against the pavement. Mesmerized, she peered around the corner, her eyes fixated on the carnage taking place just a few feet away.

Suddenly, a searing pain tore through her chest as two long blades burst forth, piercing her flesh. Blood seeped onto the transparent dress, staining it crimson. Something thick coiled around her neck, tightening its grip, while its teeth sank into her skin. Desperately, Susan fumbled with the can of mace, pointing it behind her over her shoulder. She pressed on the top, but to her shock and alarm, nothing happened.

As Susan's vision faded, a red haze encompassing her sight, the twin blades withdrew from her body, slicing in opposite directions, one of them severing her left forearm. The constricting grip around her neck was abruptly released, nearly decapitating the dying woman. Her head and chest collided with the ground, and in her final moments, Susan saw her lower half crumple and fall beside her.

With her last ounce of consciousness, Susan's gaze fell upon the can of mace, its label bearing the words, "REMOVE PIN BEFORE SHOOTING."

¤

Clarie Noble seethed with frustration. After enduring a grueling double shift at the docks and being subjected to stingy tips and pawing hands, she reluctantly agreed to give the scrawny kid a ride home. Little did she know that he would repay her kindness by vomiting all over her car. She had only just paid off her beloved Overlord blue Blupe, and now its interior reeked of Old Castaigne and stomach acid. With a deep sigh, she mustered the strength to pull the punk out of the passenger seat and guide him towards the entrance of the rundown flophouse.

As Clarie surveyed her defiled car, her attempts to clean up the mess seemed futile. The once pristine leather interior now bore unsightly stains, their color indistinguishable in the darkness that engulfed the street. Only a couple of streetlights flickered weakly, casting feeble illumination. Along the curbs, dilapidated Shantaks, Dholes, and even a Voornith with mismatched doors and tentacle-like fins jutting out from the rear bumper lined the road. Her grandfather had once owned a similar vehicle—a green one with black accents that roared menacingly as it rumbled down the street.

A nostalgic smile flickered across Clarie's face, but before it could fully form, it was abruptly cut short. A large bath towel materialized from behind, swiftly enveloping her arms, and torso, rendering her immobile. In a state of shock, she watched in disbelief as a blade burst forth from her chest, followed by another, and another. The blades repeatedly plunged in and out of her body, mercilessly tearing through her chest and abdomen. Despite the gruesome ordeal, very little blood seeped through the confines of the towel as Clarie's life gradually drained away. As darkness enveloped her, she felt strong arms catching her limp form, and then all faded into oblivion.

¤

Inspector Larry Nodens emerged from his Shantak, a trusty old car that had faithfully served him over the years. Despite its age, the vehicle had proven itself reliable, a testament to the quality craftsmanship of Sarkomand automobiles. Running his fingers along the car's fins, Larry made his way towards the gathering of officers stationed at the entrance of an alley.

Flashing blue lights illuminated the area, emanating from the Zoog patrol cars. Larry couldn't help but wonder how effective these compact vehicles would be in policing a city as vast as Dylath-Leen. It seemed impractical to him, as it took at least two of them to block off a street, and he doubted that any seasoned criminals would be deterred by such makeshift barricades. However, such matters were beyond his control and belonged to a higher echelon of decision-making.

The sentry officer standing by the yellow tape recognized Larry, the distinctive Inspector who left an indelible impression. Despite his relatively short stature of five feet six inches, Larry's years of experience on the force had earned him a reputation that couldn't be overlooked because of mere changes in standards. Clad in his customary gray overcoat, collar pulled up to meet his short, graying black hair, Larry possessed cold, piercing eyes that lurked beneath his bushy eyebrows.

Curious about the situation, Larry inquired of the commanding officer on the scene, Sergeant Matt Kirowan, "What do we have here?"

With nonchalant indifference, the veteran officer responded, "Mangled body... pieces. The M.E. is already here." As Larry moved to pass him, Sergeant Kirowan added, "He's here too."

"Of course he is," Larry muttered under his breath. He turned the corner into the alley, now illuminated by floodlights. Frank Belknap, the Medical Examiner, crouched over a scattering of body parts, meticulously examining them with an extendable pointer. Standing nearby, almost looming over Belknap's shoulder, was a tall, muscular man in a brown suit. This man, Dan Oikos, greeted Larry with a grin and swiftly intercepted the detective.

"Larry! How nice to see you again," Oikos exclaimed, extending his hand in greeting while wrapping his other arm around Larry's shoulders. Oikos was an agent of the Ravager Analysis Task Force (RATF), responsible for minimizing the public's anxiety in the wake of the Overlords' presence. "I understand your need to investigate personally, but I assure you, this is just another RAD. There's a designated offering site right over there in Shan Square."

Larry turned to Dr. Belknap and asked, "What are your initial findings?"

The Medical Examiner shook his head. "I'm not convinced this is a Ravager Attributed Death," he stated. Belknap pointed out various fragments of viscera and continued, "first, the victim wasn't exsanguinated, as evidenced by the blood that has pooled in what remains of this 'garment'," he indicated the scraps of transparent yellow plastic. "Nor was she depleted of her bodily contents."

Intrigued, Larry inquired further, "So the victim is female?"

Belknap confirmed, "Yes, you can tell by the hips. I would estimate she was in her late twenties. Her left arm appears to have been severed," he leaned in for a closer examination, "by a straight, extremely sharp object."

Agent Oikos interjected, eager to present his perspective. "What are your initial conclusions, Doctor?"

Belknap shrugged, indicating the limited evidence at hand. "It's difficult to say with certainty, given the damage caused by vermin. I've worked with less, but this case ranks among the top five in terms of difficulty."

Oikos exclaimed emphatically, "That would require an extraordinary amount of strength!"

Seeking more information, Larry pressed on, "Any form of identification?"

"Dental records will probably be necessary for identification. Her teeth are the only intact remains," Belknap replied, his expression taking on a peculiar twist. "Except for her groin area. Surprisingly, there doesn't seem to be any damage there. Oh, and there's a tattoo on the severed arm. It appears to be a lotus blossom."

With firm resolve, Larry declared to Agent Oikos, "I believe we have enough evidence to rule out a RAD. If you could kindly remove yourself from my crime scene, I would greatly appreciate it."

Oikos raised his hands in surrender. "As you wish, Inspector," he said with a broad smile. "But I'll be nearby if you need me."

Larry turned his back on the agent, his attention returning to the lifeless body before him. The victim's eyes were wide open, devoid of fear. In death, only emptiness remained.

"She wasn't afraid when she died," Larry murmured, deep in thought. "Either she knew her attacker or she was taken by surprise from behind."

Chapter 2

Nodens made his way back to the Police Presidium, where his small team of detectives awaited him. Gwen, the newest addition to the team, though occasionally scatterbrained, had proven herself to be an excellent data analyst. Alan, an older detective who had his moments of grumpiness, was known for always getting the job done. And then there was Horace, a seasoned officer who had been by Larry's side for many years. He was a tall, hairy man in his mid forties. Despite his stature and imposing looks, he was one of the best detectives in the city.

"Any updates from the initial M.E. report?" Larry inquired, knowing that the Medical Examiner would have transmitted the findings to the team by the time he returned from the crime scene.

Alan, with a nonchalant shrug, moved to another computer, searching for the information they needed.

"Sir!" Gwen called out, capturing Larry's attention. "We have another incident. It's in Leen."

Curiosity piqued, Larry pressed for more details. "Anything more specific?"

Gwen shook her head. "Not yet, but I'll see what I can find."

Larry nodded, contemplating their next move. Leen wasn't exactly the most desirable place to investigate, but he acknowledged that it was as good a lead as any.

"Let's go, Horace," Larry said, motioning for his trusted colleague to join him.

¤

Larry and Horace embarked on their journey to Leen, riding in the trusty Shantak. Leen, a bustling manufacturing center, was filled with factories, tradesmen, and the ever-present smoke from industrial activity. The Mulder Industrial Park and Scully Rail Yard dominated the heart of the area, while the Fillson Refinery stood on the polluted shores of the Sump Marsh, an unsavory swampy region near the eastern shore of the Lussian Sea.

As they arrived at the crime scene, they found Frank Belknap meticulously examining the body. A female police officer was diligently capturing photographs, while Agent Oikos observed the proceedings with his characteristic smoothness.

"Inspector, fancy meeting you here," Oikos greeted, offering a nod to Horace, who returned the gesture.

Larry immediately recognized the deceased girl as the one they had found earlier. He inquired, "How did she end up here?"

"We believe she was killed elsewhere and then dumped at this location," the officer informed them.

Belknap interjected, "The wounds are distinct, but I'm fairly certain it's the same killer."

Larry studied the victim closely. "She bears an uncanny resemblance to the Jane Doe we discovered in Tchotown this morning."

"I'm entering her fingerprints and a photo of her face into the system," the officer reported. "I'll notify you if she has a criminal record."

Larry nodded, his thoughts swirling. Horace offered a suggestion, "Perhaps they're twins? Any form of identification?"

The medical examiner shook his head. "No, nothing. However, she does have a small black lotus tattoo on her left wrist, just like the other victim. Apart from that, there's nothing remarkable."

Larry's gaze fixated on the tattoo, a flicker of recognition crossing his face. "What's with these tattoos, Horace?"

Horace shrugged. "I don't know, but one thing is clear: they're all ending up dead."

Curiosity mounting, Larry pressed on, "How did she die, doctor?"

Belknap answered, "She sustained multiple stab wounds to the chest from behind. The weapon used was likely a short sword, possibly a dagger. Or both."

Oikos chimed in, seeking clarity. "So, definitely not the work of a Ravager?"

"No," the medical examiner confirmed. "The wounds are too precise. This killer was swift, strong, and skilled, but not a Ravager."

"Thank you, doctor," Oikos acknowledged before nodding to the detectives and departing from the scene.

Larry turned to the medical examiner once more. "Is there anything else you can tell us?"

The examiner contemplated for a moment. "There is a faint scent of vomit, but it doesn't appear to be hers. Her face shows no signs of trauma, and there is no evidence of regurgitation. I'll inform you if we discover anything else."

"Appreciated," Larry replied, his mind filled with questions as they continued their investigation.

¤

Larry and Horace made their way back to the Police Presidium, contemplating their next steps.

"So, what's the plan, boss?" Horace inquired.

"I need to provide a report to the CoCID and update her on our findings so far," Larry replied.

"Alright," Horace acknowledged.

Larry proceeded directly to the CoCID's office. He rapped on the worn wooden door, adorned with a sign displaying the title "Commander, Criminal Investigations Division" and Supt. Pazia Gaunt's nameplate beneath it.

The Superintendent, a tall and attractive woman, possessed the distinctive angular features and faint bluish hue in her skin, typical of individuals born from the union of Overlords and humans who occupied high-ranking positions within the government.

"Report, Inspector Nodens!" she commanded sternly, her penetrating gaze fixed on him from behind her desk.

"We have discovered two nearly identical Jane Does. One was found this morning in Tchotown, and the other just a couple of hours ago in Leen. The only commonality between them is the presence of a black lotus tattoo on one of their arms. Both victims exhibit multiple stab wounds inflicted by a sharp weapon, possibly a dagger or short sword. The Medical Examiner has ruled out Ravager involvement in both cases," Larry explained.

"I see," Gaunt replied thoughtfully. "These killings bear the signature of an amateur, likely a fanatic inspired by the Ravagers. We will initiate an immediate manhunt for this killer."

"I believe it might be premature, CoCID. We have a few leads to pursue before alerting the killer to our investigation," Larry countered.

"Very well," Gaunt conceded. "Inspector, you are dismissed." Larry nodded in acknowledgment and exited the office, where Horace was waiting by the door.

¤

"What happened in there?" Horace asked.

"The CoCID wanted to unleash the hounds. I convinced her we should pursue other leads first," Larry explained.

"Good call, boss," Horace said.

They returned to the squad room, and Larry slumped into his chair. This case was shaping up to be a major headache, he could sense it. Just as he was about to give up for the day and head home, Gwen interjected.

"I've found something," she announced. Larry perked up, leaning in to examine the computer screen she was pointing at. It displayed a news article from two months ago.

"Pull up all the information you can find on that case!" Larry commanded. Gwen diligently typed away, and a new screen appeared with additional details.

"The victims were identified as Megan Green, 19, and Matthew Reed, 18. They were discovered eviscerated in an alley in Leen by a garbage collector. The police were baffled by the incident."

"Any similarities with our Jane Does?" Larry inquired. "Both victims sustained multiple stab wounds, possibly inflicted by a dagger or a similar weapon. However, the Medical Examiner suggested that a longer weapon might have been involved."

"Any mention of tattoos?" Larry asked.

"No tattoos were reported for either victim," Gwen responded.

"So, do we believe these cases are connected?" Horace interjected.

"I believe so. Megan Green bears a striking resemblance to our unidentified girls," Larry remarked.

Larry rose from his seat and stretched his tired limbs. "Get some rest, everyone. Tomorrow morning, I'll head over to Leen to speak with the officers who worked the crime scene. Perhaps they uncovered something valuable. Horace, inform me immediately if any new developments arise. Gwen, you've been a tremendous help, as always."

"I'll be attending the Culling with Dani tonight, so message me if anything urgent arises," Larry instructed.

"You got it, boss," Gwen acknowledged.

Larry grabbed his coat and made his way home, ready to face the challenges of the next day.

¤

"Dani, are you ready to go?" Larry called out.

Dani's head popped out from behind the bedroom door. "Just give me a second, I'm almost done," she replied, her eyes darting around anxiously.

Designed for Slaughter

Larry couldn't believe how quickly she had grown. It felt like just yesterday she was playing with her Cassilda doll around the apartment. Now she was a teenager, navigating the challenges of adolescence. The thought of her drifting away from him frightened him. He didn't want that to happen.

"We can't afford to be late, Dani! You know you'll be furious if we miss the first fight!" Larry reminded her.

"Wait up!" she responded, a touch of urgency in her voice. She disappeared back into her room. After a moment, Dani emerged fully dressed with a bag slung over her shoulder.

"You won't be allowed to bring that bag into the arena, Dani," Larry pointed out.

She glanced down at the bag and then back up at him. "Oh, shit," she exclaimed. She placed the bag down and quickly rummaged through it before giving a nod.

"Okay, let's go."

They hailed a taxi and headed to the New Dylath Arena in the Downtown District for the Culling. It was a weekly event where two dozen young men fought until only one remained standing. Larry had managed to secure tickets in the splatter zone, which was just behind the barrier and occasionally got showered with blood. It was also a prime spot for collecting souvenirs.

Dani seemed more excited than he had ever seen her.

"Are you excited, sweetheart?" Larry asked.

"I am! I can't wait!" Dani exclaimed.

"You seem a bit tense. Just try to relax. You'll have plenty of opportunities to cheer," Larry advised.

Dani let out a huff but nodded in agreement.

"What do you feel like eating?" Larry inquired.

Dani shrugged. "I don't know. Whatever you want is fine."

Larry ordered a bucket of ribs and a large side of blupe. He got a Camilla Pop for Dani and a Nyogtha beer for himself, even though he wasn't usually a fan of the red stuff. It was the only option available.

They found their seats, and Dani stood up, enthusiastically cheering as the combatants entered the arena. The people around them seemed to be acquainted with each other, and a couple of rows away, someone had brought a crying baby.

"I can't wait for the blood!" Dani exclaimed, bouncing up and down in her seat. As if on cue, the arena lights turned red, and the fighters engaged each other.

The carnage unfolded before their eyes. Some wielded spiked armor, others swung giant hammers, and a few had metal claws embedded in their gloves. The Splatter Zone swiftly became drenched in blood, while the splatter guard dripped with entrails, bone fragments, and gore.

Larry and Dani indulged in their food and drinks during the fights, completely engrossed in the spectacle. By the end, they had forgotten all about the crying baby. Dani's cheers were the loudest, and Larry told her so.

"I love the blood!" she screamed with exhilaration. When the last fighter triumphantly held up his opponent's bloody head for the crowd to see, Dani leaped to her feet and cheered with all her might.

The victorious fighter noticed her and playfully tossed his opponent's shattered helmet over the splatter barrier, winking at Dani. She caught it and proudly displayed it to the roaring crowd.

Arm in arm, they exited the arena, their clothes and faces painted in blood. "That was incredible!" Dani exclaimed.

Larry nodded, unsure of what to say.

Dani looked at him expectantly. "I want to be a warrior!" she declared.

Let's hope it never comes to that, Larry thought to himself. He smiled and nodded again, hailing a cab as they headed home.

¤

They climbed into the back of a taxi, and the driver glanced at them through the rearview mirror. "Just came from there, huh?" he asked. Larry nodded. "First time?"

"No, not really," Larry replied.

The driver chuckled. "I can tell. You seem cool with it. Most people aren't. They scream and cry and make a fuss. I usually take the longer route back downtown to avoid the craziness. Hey, if you're up for it, how about going to the Snuff Stadium?"

"Not tonight," Larry responded. "We've had enough excitement for one day."

"Alrighty then," the driver said, pulling out into traffic. Dani turned to Larry, curiosity in her eyes. "What's the Snuff Stadium?"

"It's like the Culling, but with unusual animals," Larry explained.

"Cool!" Dani exclaimed, and Larry smiled.

The rest of the cab ride was quiet. Larry looked out the window, the city lights creating a dreamlike ambiance against the dark sky. When they arrived at their apartment in the Ivy City District, Larry paid the driver, and they stepped out of the car.

As they entered the apartment, Dani immediately went to the window, pressing her face against the glass and gazing outside. "Can we go up to the roof?" she asked eagerly.

"We need to clean up and then it's bedtime," Larry replied.

"Aw..." Dani whined, disappointed.

Larry headed to the bathroom, running water over his hands and splashing some on his face, observing his tired reflection in the mirror. "I definitely need some sleep," he muttered to himself.

He undressed, tossing his clothes into the hamper in the corner of the bathroom. "A hot shower will do wonders," he thought.

Larry stepped into the shower, allowing the warm water to wash away the blood and the weariness from his body. He closed his eyes, feeling the water cascade down his back and drain away the fatigue.

After finishing his shower, he turned off the water and wrapped himself in a towel from the rack. Just as he returned to the bedroom, there was a knock on the door. He opened it, motioning for Dani to enter. After a moment of hesitation, she joined him.

Larry walked over to the bed and sat down at the end, and Dani stood in the middle of the room, surveying her surroundings. "Can I sit with you?" she asked.

"Of course," Larry replied with a warm smile.

Dani made her way to the bed and sat down next to him. They both sat in silence, unsure of how to break it. Dani looked up at her father, and he met her gaze.

"What's on your mind, sweetie?" Larry asked gently.

"I just don't understand boys," Dani admitted, her voice filled with uncertainty.

"What don't you understand?" Larry inquired, his tone compassionate.

Dani shrugged her shoulders, looking down. "Everything?" she said with a mix of frustration and vulnerability.

Larry couldn't help but chuckle softly, though he quickly realized Dani wasn't amused. "I know it's not funny," he said, trying to reassure her. "It's just... it's normal, Dani. You're at an age where your world is expanding rapidly. Boys, the Schola, Selection Prep—it's a lot to take in. Take it one thing at a time, and you'll figure it out."

Dani let out a sigh and managed a smile. "Good night, Dani," Larry said.

"Good night, Dad," she replied, heading back to her own bed.

Larry switched off the lights and settled into the darkness. His eyes grew heavy, and he drifted off to sleep, hoping that Dani would navigate the complexities of adolescence with confidence and self-discovery.

Chapter 3

Alison Craven stood anxiously inside the entrance to the dimly lit warehouse. The informant had insisted on meeting in this secluded location, away from prying eyes. She couldn't help but feel uneasy in the Waterfront District, especially at night, but leaving her four-year-old daughter, Molly, alone at home was out of the question. With no one available to look after Molly at this hour, Alison had no choice but to bring her along. She glanced down at Molly, who clutched her hand tightly.

They entered through the side door, which had been left unlocked as the informant had promised. Alison carefully avoided the surveillance cameras and the occasional security guard on patrol, following the informant's instructions. Inside the warehouse, she paced nervously, glancing at her watch repeatedly. The informant was late. Should she leave? No, she couldn't afford to give up on this opportunity. The informant claimed to have evidence that her client was involved in money laundering for Lengite slavers. Alison couldn't let them get away with it. Reporting it to the authorities would implicate her as an accomplice, since she had been responsible for their bookkeeping.

As she was lost in her thoughts, a sudden noise startled Alison. She turned abruptly, squinting in the dim light. A figure emerged from the shadows, carrying a large duffel bag. It appeared humanoid, but its features were obscured.

"Are you 'the dream maker'?" Alison asked cautiously, her voice betraying her unease. The figure nodded silently. "Do you have the documentation? I can't take any action without concrete proof of their crimes," she continued, her voice filled with urgency. Once again, the figure nodded. "Okay, how should we proceed?"

Reaching into the bag, the figure retrieved a stack of papers tied together with a string. Without a word, it tossed the bundle onto the floor between them.

Alison's brow furrowed as she knelt, her skirted suit pooling around her. She reached out to grab the bundle, only to realize it was heavier than she had expected. In her nervousness, it slipped from her fingers, hitting the ground with a metallic clink. Before she could react, a mysterious substance sprayed from inside the bundle, enveloping her face. A moment of dizziness overcame her, and Alison collapsed to the floor, unconscious.

¤

When Larry woke up in the morning, he glanced at himself in the mirror and took a moment to gather his thoughts. He gently knocked on Dani's bedroom door, but there was no response except for the soft sound of her snoring. Larry entered the room and sat down on the edge of the bed, looking at his still-sleeping daughter.

"It's time to get ready, Dani. You can't be late for the Schola," Larry said, his voice filled with a mixture of concern and encouragement. Dani stirred, slowly opening her eyes and focusing on her father. She sat up, stretching her arms.

"Dad, I love you," Dani whispered, leaning over to give him a kiss on the cheek. Larry smiled and returned the affection by kissing her on the forehead.

"I love you too, sweetie," Larry replied, his voice filled with warmth. He nodded, stood up, and made his way back to the bathroom. Taking a quick shower, he dressed for the day before heading to the living room.

As Larry entered the living room, he found Dani waiting, her uniform bedecked with the ribbons and awards she had earned, ready to go. She had gathered her belongings and was eager to start her day at the Schola. Larry put on his shoes, grabbed his keys, and walked towards the door, with Dani following closely behind.

Together, they got into the car, and Larry drove Dani to the Schola. The training academy seemed like a mysterious place to Larry, where children entered and emerged as servants of the Overlords. He was not privy to the details of their curriculum, and Dani was bound by secrecy. Attendance was mandatory, and as an agent of the Overlords himself, Larry understood the importance of setting a good example for the ordinary citizens.

"Goodbye, Dad," Dani said as she got out of the car, ready to embark on her day of learning and growth.

"Take care, Dani. Be your best," Larry replied, his voice filled with both pride and fatherly concern. He watched her walk through the gates of the Schola, his gaze lingering for a moment before he turned the car around and drove away, his thoughts consumed by a mix of emotions.

¤

Larry parked his car outside the Police Presidium, a grand building designed to resemble an Akkadian fortress. It served as the city hall and the central hub for the police department. Stepping out of the vehicle, Larry made his way towards the entrance, his footsteps determined.

Inside the bustling building, officers moved about with focused energy. Larry navigated through the corridors until he reached the squad room, where his team of detectives gathered, engrossed in conversation and the aroma of freshly brewed coffee. Gwen was engaged in a discussion with another colleague.

Larry approached her with a sense of urgency. He leaned in slightly and addressed her, his voice firm yet composed.

"Gwen," Larry called out, capturing her attention.

She turned towards him, her expression transitioning into one of attentive professionalism.

"Sir," Gwen replied respectfully.

Larry wasted no time and got straight to the point, his eyes fixed on Gwen's.

"Any new developments on our Jane Does?" he inquired, his voice carrying a hint of anticipation.

Gwen's face revealed a tinge of frustration as she responded, her dedication apparent.

"Nothing yet, sir," Gwen replied, her determination unwavering.

Larry nodded, acknowledging the challenges they faced, but emphasizing their shared commitment.

"Keep at it. We'll uncover the identities of these women," he instructed, his voice exuding confidence and assurance.

"Yes, sir," Gwen affirmed, her resolve echoing in her response.

Larry's attention then turned to Alan.

"Alan, any progress in establishing connections between our victims and the individuals involved in the Green/Reed case?" Larry inquired, his tone reflecting both curiosity and determination.

Alan shook his head, a tinge of disappointment in his voice.

"Not yet, sir," Alan admitted, his dedication clear in his response.

Larry's gaze shifted to his desk, where a stack of papers, topped by a copy of the police report on that cold case, awaited his attention. He contemplated the ongoing investigations, knowing that every piece of information held the potential to bring closure to those affected.

Taking a moment to gather his thoughts, Larry prepared himself to delve into the complexities that lay before him, ready to lead his team towards answers and resolution.

¤

The detective's report on the incident was disappointingly concise, encompassing only two brief pages. It lacked the comprehensive details Larry hoped for, providing only the bare essentials of the case.

The circumstances appeared rather straightforward. A group of eight teenagers had illicitly gained access to the enigmatic Leen monolith, one of the colossal obsidian towers that materialized upon the Overlords' arrival, seeking a clandestine location for their drinking escapade. Their presence had been discovered by a vigilant security guard, prompting the subsequent involvement of the teens' concerned parents and their subsequent transport to the hospital.

Within this group, two individuals named Green and Reed had suffered multiple puncture wounds to their chests, inflicted from behind. The Ravager Analysis Task Force initially sought to classify these deaths as Ravager Attributed Deaths, speculating the involvement of the otherworldly alien predators. However, the medical examiner's analysis determined that the wounds possessed a remarkable cleanliness, incongruous with the typical modus operandi of the Ravagers. Subsequently, the investigation into the case had abruptly halted, with Larry's team never assigned to pursue further leads.

A knock on his office door interrupted Larry's concentration, prompting him to lift his gaze. Horace, stood at the entrance, apologetic yet brimming with urgency.

"Sorry to interrupt, sir," Horace spoke, his voice respectful.

Larry's curiosity piqued, and he motioned for Horace to proceed.

"What's up?" Larry inquired, his tone eagerly.

"We've just received a new case, sir. A woman stumbled upon a body while walking her dog," Horace explained.

Larry's eyebrows furrowed as he absorbed the information, his mind already racing with possibilities.

"Where did this occur?" Larry queried, his voice betraying a hint of concern.

"In a ditch nestled amidst several warehouses in the Waterfront District," Horace replied promptly.

"Let's head there without delay," Larry declared with a resolute tone.

"Yes, sir," Horace affirmed, his demeanor reflecting their shared commitment to upholding justice and unraveling the mysteries that lay ahead.

¤

Arriving at the scene, Larry and Horace were met by two uniformed officers standing near the lifeless body. The gruesome scene unfolded before them—a woman whose throat had been savagely torn apart, accompanied by a deep slash across her wrist.

Dan Oikos was crouched next to the corpse, engaged in conversation with the medical examiner. As Larry approached, Oikos rose to his feet, acknowledging their arrival.

"Inspector," Dan greeted Larry respectfully.

"Oikos," Larry replied, his attention fixated on the deceased woman before him.

Larry turned to the medical examiner, Dr. Belknap.

"What can you tell me about her, Frank?" Larry inquired, his voice laden with a sense of urgency.

"Not much at the moment," Dr. Belknap responded, his tone laced with frustration. "I couldn't find any matches for her in my database. I'm currently running her fingerprints for identification."

Larry nodded in understanding, acknowledging the limitations faced by the medical examiner in the early stages of their investigation. Dr. Belknap then stood up, signaling the conclusion of his immediate duties.

"I'm finished here. Should you require further assistance, you can find me at my office two blocks east," Dr. Belknap informed them before departing.

As Larry observed the young woman's lifeless form once more, he took note of her features—a mane of long blonde hair and an expensive suit, hinting at a certain level of affluence.

An approaching uniformed officer approached Larry.

"Inspector," the officer addressed him. "We've already begun our efforts to secure surveillance footage and interview the warehouse personnel. We've identified a security guard responsible for monitoring the cameras during the night."

Larry contemplated the information presented, piecing together a preliminary understanding of the situation.

"So, what are your initial thoughts, sir?" Horace inquired, his voice brimming with curiosity.

Larry's gaze shifted from the lifeless body to Horace, his expression reflecting a combination of concern and determination.

"She bears a striking resemblance to our previous Jane Does and Megan Green. It appears we're dealing with a serial killer," Larry concluded, his voice tinged with gravity.

Horace absorbed the gravity of the situation, poised to take the next necessary steps.

"What's our plan, sir?" Horace asked, seeking guidance.

Larry's mind was already set on the next course of action.

"We'll focus on acquiring and scrutinizing the video surveillance footage," Larry declared, his tone resolute.

"Yes, sir," Horace affirmed, recognizing the significance of this crucial step in their pursuit of justice.

With their purpose clear, Larry and Horace made their way back to the Police Presidium, boarding the Shantak to return to the headquarters, ready to dive deeper into the investigation that lay ahead.

Chapter 4

Larry and Horace dedicated the next four hours to closely scrutinizing the grainy footage from the warehouse surveillance cameras. Unfortunately, the footage offered little in the way of useful information. Several individuals, large and hunched, entered the area, but only one person was captured leaving with a bag—presumably containing the woman's lifeless body.

Fixated on the image of the man carrying the bag, Larry examined it intently. The man appeared to have regular human proportions, distinct from the typical dockworkers, and was dressed in a cap, hoodie, and blue jeans. Despite the efforts, the security guard at the gate could not positively identify the individual based on the footage.

Realizing the importance of identifying the man with the bag, Larry called upon Gwen for help.

"Gwen! See if you can find a match for the man seen carrying the bag," Larry instructed, a sense of urgency underlying his words.

"Okay," Gwen responded, ready to delve into the task at hand. "Give me a minute."

Larry patiently waited as Gwen meticulously combed through the extensive police records. However, despite her thorough search, Gwen was unable to uncover any relevant results.

"He could very well be our prime suspect. He's the sole individual seen leaving the area," Gwen pointed out. "Furthermore, he stands out from the others as he doesn't resemble a typical dockworker."

"We need to find out his identity," Larry asserted.

"I'm on it," Gwen affirmed, determined to dig deeper and find the answers they sought.

An additional hour elapsed as Gwen sifted through the DLPD databases. Eventually, she emerged with a potential lead.

"I think I've found something," Gwen announced. "There's a man named Tomas Nivorio who was apprehended last night for public drunkenness. He was carrying a bag identical to the one the killer had."

"Where is he now?" Larry inquired, his voice laced with a sense of anticipation.

"He's currently being held in the cells," Gwen revealed.

"Good. I'll go speak to him," Larry declared decisively.

Making his way to the holding cells, Larry recognized Tomas from the photograph in his file.

"Bring him to an interrogation room!" Larry commanded, his tone authoritative as he prepared to extract the truth from the potential suspect.

¤

Larry positioned himself across the table from Tomas, establishing a confrontational yet controlled presence.

"Hello, Tomas," Larry greeted, his tone firm but not hostile. "I'm Inspector Larry Nodens."

Tomas nodded nervously, his apprehension evident.

"I... I didn't kill that woman," Tomas immediately asserted, his voice trembling.

Larry maintained his focused gaze, unaffected by Tomas' denial.

"We have video evidence of you exiting the warehouse with a large bag. Care to explain what was inside?" Larry inquired, his tone probing.

"Just some stuff. The cops took it," Tomas replied, his response lacking in detail.

Larry leaned forward, his expression stern. "I need you to be more specific, Tomas. You can choose whether we have a friendly or unfriendly conversation," Larry asserted, leaving no room for ambiguity.

Tomas remained silent, avoiding eye contact by directing his gaze downwards, fixating on the table.

Larry's voice took on a more pressing tone as he continued, determined to elicit a response. "Tell me about the drugs," Larry prodded, his words demanding answers.

Tomas seemed increasingly anxious, his nerves palpable.

"Why are you reluctant to divulge information about the drugs?" Larry pressed further, seeking to uncover the truth.

Tomas finally looked up, his terror-stricken eyes meeting Larry's unwavering gaze. "Fine," Tomas relented, his voice wavering. "It was just... drugs."

Larry pushed for more details, not content with the evasive response. "What kind of drugs?" he pressed, intensifying the pressure.

"I don't know... Just... drugs," Tomas stammered, his nervousness growing.

Larry sensed the need to change the line of questioning, honing in on a different aspect of the situation. "Let's discuss the bag itself," Larry shifted his focus, his voice unwavering.

Tomas hesitated before responding, surprised by the change in topic. "It was just... a duffel bag," Tomas replied, his voice strained.

Larry's suspicion grew as he narrowed down the possibilities. "Was it sealed or open?" Larry probed, his voice tinged with an edge.

Tomas nodded in affirmation, confirming Larry's suspicions. "Yeah, it was sealed," Tomas confirmed, his voice subdued.

Seizing the opportunity, Larry abruptly released his grip on Tomas' handcuffed wrists, giving him a momentary respite from pain.

"What the hell is your problem?" Tomas exclaimed, his anguish clear.

Larry leaned back slightly, maintaining an intense presence. "You need to start telling me the truth, Tomas. There's more to this than you're letting on," Larry demanded, his tone seething with intensity.

"I don't know anything about a woman in a suit," Tomas denied, his fear mounting.

Larry persisted, increasing the pressure on Tomas. "You're still lying," Larry asserted firmly. "Tell me what you know about the woman in the suit."

Tomas met Larry's piercing gaze, sweat forming on his forehead, a mixture of fear and desperation in his eyes.

"When was your last fix, Tomas?" Larry inquired compassionately.

Confusion filled Tomas' face as he struggled to comprehend the sudden change.

"What?" Tomas responded, his voice tinged with bewilderment.

Larry repeated the question with conviction, emphasizing its significance.

"When was the last time you took drugs?" Larry pressed, his voice demanding answers.

"I don't know," Tomas admitted reluctantly, wincing as he spoke.

Larry continued his relentless pursuit of the truth, probing deeper into Tomas' memory.

"How long has it been?" Larry persisted, urging Tomas to recall the details.

Tomas hesitated before responding, his voice faltering.

"Three days," Tomas admitted, his vulnerability laid bare.

Larry seized upon this admission, recognizing the potential significance.

"You must be pretty strung out," Larry observed, his voice laden with implication.

"Yeah," Tomas replied, his tone reflecting the truth in Larry's statement.

Unyielding in his pursuit, Larry pressed on, intensifying the interrogation.

"Do you remember what you were doing three nights ago?" Larry interrogated, his tone unyielding.

Tomas paused, attempting to recollect his memories.

"Yeah, I do," Tomas eventually responded.

Larry seized the opening, eager for more information.

"What were you doing?" Larry pressed, his voice insistent.

"I was... I was at the..." Tomas began, his words interrupted by a cry of pain as Larry increased the pressure on his wrists.

"Tell me where you were!" Larry demanded, his voice filled with urgency.

"I was at the Black Cat Bar!" Tomas exclaimed, his words punctuated by a mixture of pain and desperation.

"Keep talking," Larry commanded, sensing that they were on the cusp of a breakthrough.

"That's all I did! I was just at the bar, got drunk, and got a ride home," Tomas continued, his voice strained.

"From who?" Larry inquired, his voice demanding precision.

"From one of the barmaids," Tomas responded, his voice tinged with uncertainty.

Larry recognized the significance of this connection, seeking to extract further details.

"Which one?" Larry probed, his voice expectant.

"I don't know her name. She was... nice," Tomas confessed, his memory failing him.

Larry shifted tactics, placing photographs of the victims on the table, presenting Tomas with a visual cue.

"Look at these photos. Is any of them the barmaid?" Larry inquired, his voice holding a glimmer of hope.

Tomas studied the photographs intently, his gaze lingering on each image.

"This one," Tomas eventually pointed to a specific photograph, with certainty.

"Are you sure? Is she the woman who gave you a ride home?" Larry questioned, his voice demanding absolute certainty.

Tomas nodded, his belief unwavering.

"What was her name?" Larry pressed, his voice probing yet hopeful.

"I don't know. I never caught her name," Tomas admitted, with regret.

"Did you mention this to the police?" Larry asked, his tone expressing frustration.

"No. They never asked," Tomas confessed, his voice filled with a sense of missed opportunity.

Allowing the information to settle, Larry gave Tomas some time to reflect.

"I'm going to leave you here to think. Try to remember anything else. I'll be back later," Larry declared, rising from his seat and exiting the room.

Making his way into the adjacent observation room, Larry joined Horace and Gwen, who were awaiting his update.

"Well?" Horace inquired eagerly.

"He mentioned that one of the Jane Does worked at a place called the Black Cat Bar. Gwen, gather files on all the bar's employees," Larry commanded, his gaze fixed on Gwen.

"On it," Gwen affirmed, and left to carry out the task assigned to her.

¤

Larry and his team dedicated the following hours to meticulously examining the files of each employee at the Black Cat bar. They systematically ruled out male employees and several others, narrowing down their focus to two women who seemed to be potential matches.

Horace expressed his uncertainty. "Are you sure that one's her?" he questioned, seeking reassurance.

"Pretty sure," Larry replied, confidence resonating in his voice. "Her name was Claire Noble."

Seeking further information, Gwen interjected, "Should I find out if Claire has a twin?"

Larry nodded decisively. "Yes, let's dig into that."

Gwen swiftly obtained the file, printing it out and handing it over to Larry. He opened Claire's file and began reading through its contents.

"This document states that Claire was part of a genetic test. They're clones! Two out of six. I suspect the third victim might be another clone," Larry revealed, his voice laced with intrigue.

Gwen, taken aback by this revelation, voiced her surprise. "Cloned? Is that even possible?"

Larry contemplated the profound implications of this discovery. "With the capabilities of the Overlords? Who knows what they can do?"

As Larry delved deeper into the files, he found himself questioning the extent of the Overlords' influence on humanity.

"To fully investigate this cloning project, we'll need permission. I'll reach out to the CoCID," Larry declared, determined to uncover the truth behind the cloning operation.

Understanding the gravity of the situation, Horace and Gwen nodded in agreement, ready to assist Larry in his pursuit of the truth.

¤

Larry made his way to the office of the CoCID, the tension building within him. As he entered, she glanced up from her desk, her expression neutral.

"Inspector Nodens, report," she said, her tone devoid of emotion.

"We have a third victim, suggesting a serial killer. All the victims are clones who were part of an experimental project. Our priority is to gather information about this project and locate the remaining three clones," Larry explained, his voice steady.

"Clones?" the CoCID responded, seemingly surprised by the revelation.

"Yes, I have all the pertinent information here," Larry said, handing over the file containing the details of the case. The CoCID quickly skimmed through the contents, her face impassive.

"We don't yet know the identity of the killer, and accessing the project's records is crucial. However, it falls under the purview of the Overlord Authority."

The CoCID stared at him, her gaze unwavering. After a momentary pause, she took a sip of her coffee, a sinister grin forming on her lips. "Why don't you simply ask your minder for assistance? Agent Oikos has connections with the OA and can likely arrange access for you. He may already have the authorization... and the information."

Larry's apprehension surfaced as he responded, "I'd prefer to avoid involvement from the RATF in my investigation. If I seek Agent Oikos' help, he'll accompany me on all my inquiries, potentially impeding progress. He was present at all the crime scenes when I arrived and was ready to classify them all as RADs."

The CoCID scrutinized Larry, her gaze piercing. "I understand," she stated. "So, you don't trust our sister service to safeguard the interests of the Overlords and the citizens of Dylath-Leen?"

"Not that, sir," Larry stumbled, a sharp pain pulsating through his head as her penetrating gaze intensified. "I believe an independent assessment of the situation would better serve the interests of the Overlords and the citizens."

Pazia Gaunt's face twisted into an unpleasant smile, a sign of satisfaction or possibly scheming. "Very well, Inspector. I will submit the request for access to the project records."

"Thank you, CoCID," Larry expressed gratefully.

"You're dismissed," she said curtly.

Larry saluted and turned to leave, his hand resting on the doorknob. Before he opened it, the Superintendent's voice halted him. "Leave it open."

Larry obeyed, leaving the door slightly ajar as he exited the CoCID's office, his mind already racing with anticipation for the next steps in the investigation.

¤

Larry entered the living room to find Dani engrossed in her phone, her attention fixated on the screen. He approached her and greeted her with a question.

"Hey, Dani," he said. "What are you doing?"

Dani responded nonchalantly, not bothering to look up from her phone. "Nothing."

Curiosity piqued, Larry inquired further. "Who were you talking to?"

"Just... a friend," Dani replied vaguely.

Larry couldn't help but feel a pang of jealousy creeping in. He attempted to steer the conversation towards a different topic. "What did you learn at the Schola today? You rarely have homework. When I was in school, we had homework every night."

Dani dismissed his inquiry with a teasing remark, finally glancing up from her phone. "That's because you're old."

Larry chuckled, trying to bridge the gap between them. "Old? I'm only forty."

Dani's response was apathetic.

"There's not much to tell. I go to class, I come home. You work all day, you come home. You never tell me about your day."

Larry felt a twinge of guilt as he realized he hadn't been sharing much about his own life.

Dani's tone softened, expressing a desire to connect. "I'm sorry. I just want to hear about your day."

Larry nodded, understanding her need for engagement, but the conversation quickly dwindled. Dani returned her focus to her phone, leaving Larry to sigh and retreat to the kitchen to prepare dinner.

As he rummaged through the fridge, Larry sought to entice Dani's appetite. "Dani, do you want dinner?"

"I'm not hungry," she replied dismissively.

"Please, hun, it's been a long day. Just something simple," Larry pleaded.

Reluctantly, Dani declined the offer, engrossed in her phone. Resigned, Larry began heating some leftover stir-fry for himself. He ate his meal while watching TV, occasionally stealing glances at Dani, who remained absorbed in her digital world.

Completing his dinner, Larry returned to the kitchen to clean up. Upon finishing the task, he headed back to the living room in search of relaxation. The sound of buzzing filled the air, prompting Dani to abruptly shut off her phone.

Observing the time, Larry spoke with gentle firmness. "Dani, it's past ten. Time for bed."

Dani pouted and protested, "Do we have to? I'm not tired. And I don't feel well."

Concerned, Larry inquired further. "You don't feel well? What's wrong?"

"I'm nauseous, and my head hurts," Dani said.

Slightly frustrated, Larry gently reproached her, suspecting the cause of her discomfort. "Probably from spending hours looking at your phone."

Defensively, Dani rebutted, "It's only been an hour!"

"Dani, I know it's been more than that," Larry responded with understanding.

Reluctantly, Dani conceded, "Fine. I'm going to bed."

"Alright. Don't forget to brush your teeth," Larry reminded her.

Rolling her eyes, Dani left for the bathroom. Larry heard the sound of water running briefly before she retreated to her room, closing the door behind her. Exhausted, he sank onto the couch.

The television was still on, playing a mindless reality show they both disliked. Larry seized the opportunity to switch it to something more engaging. Suddenly, a thumping noise emanated from Dani's room, jolting Larry into action.

Alarmed, he rushed to Dani's door and knocked urgently. "Dani, are you alright?!"

No response. Larry cautiously opened the door and discovered Dani lying on her bed, seemingly asleep. He breathed a sigh of relief, entering the room and gently closing the door behind him. Sitting down beside Dani, he gazed at her serene face.

Concerned for her well-being, Larry placed a hand on her forehead and detected a slight fever. Realizing the importance of her medication, he got up and went to her dresser, opening the top drawer. Retrieving the hypospray, he injected the prescribed compound into Dani's neck. She stirred momentarily but remained sound asleep.

Larry wished he knew more about the medication, but it was prescribed by the Schola to address any afflictions Dani experienced, whether physical or mental. Exhausted, he retired to bed and eventually drifted off to sleep, hoping that Dani would awaken feeling better in the morning.

Chapter 5

In the morning, Larry prepared breakfast for both of them and sat down at the table to eat. Concerned about Dani's well-being, he initiated a conversation.

"How are you feeling?" he asked, his eyes fixed on her.

"I'm fine," Dani responded, hastily finishing her breakfast. She then rushed off to the bathroom. Larry heard running water for a few minutes before she reappeared, grabbing her bag in a hurry.

A short while later, Larry drove Dani to the Schola. As they made their way, he noticed her anxiety and decided to address it.

"What's wrong, Dani? Is something going on at the Schola today?" he inquired, his voice filled with genuine concern.

Dani's response carried a sense of uncertainty. "I dunno, I guess."

Observing her left hand trembling, Larry peered into her eyes and detected fear reflected in them. He gently squeezed her hand for reassurance.

"Can you tell me about it?" he asked, hoping to ease her worries.

"They said I have to go back," Dani finally disclosed, her voice quivering.

"Back where?" Larry probed, trying to understand the situation.

"To the room," Dani replied, gripping her father's arm tightly.

Larry's brow furrowed with concern. "What room?"

"Room 523," Dani uttered, her fear intensifying as she clung to her father's arm.

Seeking more information, Larry persisted, "Can you tell me about Room 523?"

Dani shook her head, her fear rendering her unable to share the details. Sensing her distress, Larry tried to offer some guidance.

"If they say you have to, then do as you are instructed. I'll see you tonight," he assured her, attempting to instill a sense of trust and support.

"Okay," Dani responded, her voice still trembling. She embraced her father tightly before joining a group of girls her age. Larry watched them enter the Schola building, his worry lingering. He then drove off, heading towards the Police Presidium, where his responsibilities awaited him.

¤

"Any new developments, team? What about those tattoos, Alan?" Larry inquired, his gaze shifting to Alan, one of his investigators.

"We traced the origin of the needles used for the tattoos, boss," Alan replied. "The tattoo parlor informed us that they sold them to an individual with a peculiar accent."

"What kind of accent are we talking about? Parg? Celephaian?" Larry questioned, trying to narrow down the possibilities.

"Neither, sir. It was more like... a hissing sound. The parlor owner couldn't identify it precisely, but he described it as a hiss," Alan explained.

"Excellent work, Alan," Larry commended him for the progress made.

"Perhaps it could be a Lengite," Horace interjected, offering his insight.

"A Lengite?" Alan repeated, slightly taken aback. "You mean those people who wear robes with hoods?"

Larry nodded. "Yes, Alan. They're part of the community and have been granted the freedom to conceal their physical features by the Overlords."

Larry pondered for a moment, realizing the potential implications. "Well, let's not jump to conclusions. We need more concrete evidence."

"So, what's next, boss?" Horace asked expectantly.

"I need to update the CoCID," Larry said.

¤

Larry proceeded directly to Superintendent Gaunt's office. The CoCID looked up from her desk as he entered.

"Inspector Nodens, report," she said with a composed demeanor.

Larry took a moment to gather his thoughts before providing the update. "Two of the victims were found with Lengite tattoos, indicating a possible connection to the Lengite community. Additionally, we have identified two of the victims. Claire Noble, one of the waitresses at the Black Cat Bar, was found in an alleyway under similar circumstances as the other victims."

The CoCID listened attentively, her gaze fixed on Larry. "We will need a comprehensive list of all personnel who worked at the bar. I will assign my best team to gather that information."

"Actually, we have already gone through the personnel files. We have a person of interest in custody who positively identified Claire Noble as one of the waitresses."

The CoCID's eyes narrowed, indicating her curiosity. "You already have a person of interest? What is his name?"

"His name is Tomas Nivorio, a low-level alcoholic and drug addict."

Before Larry could provide further details, the CoCID interrupted him abruptly. "That will be all, Inspector," she said, dismissively.

Somewhat taken aback by the sudden dismissal, Larry nodded and turned to leave the office, the door closing behind him. He understood that the Superintendent had other matters to attend to, but he couldn't shake off the feeling that she was withholding something. Nevertheless, he needed to focus on the investigation at hand and gather more evidence to build a solid case against Tomas Nivorio.

"We take a break, team," Larry declared as he returned to the squad room. "Lunch is on me. We all need some time to recharge and regroup."

His words were met with smiles and gratitude from the team members. They expressed their appreciation before leaving the office together, looking forward to a well-deserved lunch break.

¤

Later, Larry and his team found themselves in a local café. They placed their orders and engaged in casual conversation as they waited for their meals to arrive.

During their time at the café, Larry couldn't help but notice a beautiful waitress who attended to their table. His cheeks flushed slightly, and he quickly averted his gaze. However, as she passed by with a plate of fries, their eyes met again, and she offered him a warm smile.

Feeling a mix of emotions, Larry glanced down at his half-empty beer glass, momentarily lost in his thoughts. When he looked up once more, he found the waitress still looking at him, her smile captivating him. A shiver ran down his spine, stirring a sense of both excitement and guilt within him. He instinctively looked away again, trying to regain his composure.

Gwen, observing the interaction, broke the silence. "I think she likes you," she remarked playfully.

Larry sighed softly, feeling conflicted. "I can't," he confessed.

Surprised, Gwen inquired, "Why not?"

"I'm married," Larry admitted, his voice tinged with sadness.

Realizing her misstep, Gwen's tone softened. "Oh, right. You mentioned your wife before. How is she?"

A flicker of pain crossed Larry's face. "She's been gone for eight years. Taken by the Overlords," he replied with a hint of sorrow.

Gwen offered her condolences. "I'm sorry to hear that."

Larry shrugged, trying to maintain a sense of resilience. "Don't worry about it," he replied, raising his glass. "Let's drink."

Gwen clinked her glass against Larry's, and they both took a sip. Larry then motioned for another beer, and it was swiftly brought to the table. After settling the bill, they gathered their belongings and made their way back to the police precinct, ready to continue their work.

¤

When Larry arrived at the Police Presidium, he Larry entered the interrogation room where Tomas was seated, appearing frail and unwell. His complexion was pale, with a hint of gray. Larry approached him with a concerned expression.

"You don't look too good, Tomas," Larry remarked.

Tomas nodded weakly. "I don't feel too good, yeah."

Larry leaned in, his voice filled with genuine concern. "Did you take anything?"

Tomas grimaced. "I have a headache. Got a bad stomach ache."

Larry's attention was drawn to the small, pin-sized holes on Tomas' forearms as he rolled up his sleeves. He furrowed his brow, observing the marks.

"I bet they're itchy too," Larry noted.

Tomas tried to scratch his arms absentmindedly. "Yeah, they're itchy."

Larry's curiosity grew. "Any idea what it could be?"

Tomas shook his head. "Nope."

Larry pressed further, his tone firm but compassionate. "Have you remembered anything else about the other night?"

Tomas paused, closing his eyes in concentration. "I remember there was a lot of noise, yeah."

Larry leaned closer, urging Tomas to recall more details. "What kind of noise?"

"People shouting, yeah," Tomas responded, his voice growing distant. "And guns, I think."

Larry took a deep breath, hoping for additional information. "Anything else?"

"That's about it, yeah," Tomas admitted, sounding disappointed with his lack of substantial memories.

Feeling a mix of frustration and sympathy, Larry stood up from his seat. "I'll have the guard bring you something."

"Thanks, yeah," Tomas murmured gratefully.

As Larry exited the room, he encountered Superintendent Gaunt waiting outside. She wore a concerned expression on her face.

"What's the story?" Gaunt inquired.

"He remembers shouting and gunfire. That's it," Larry replied, a tinge of disappointment evident in his voice.

Gaunt frowned, clearly expecting more fruitful information. "That's all?"

Larry nodded solemnly. "That's all, for now."

The CoCID informed him of her imminent departure. "I have to go. Come see me when you have something substantial."

"Of course," Larry replied dutifully as he watched Gaunt walk away.

Feeling the weight of the investigation on his shoulders, Larry took a brief break. He made his way to the canteen, hoping to clear his mind and gather his thoughts.

¤

Larry purchased a Celephaian coffee from the canteen and found a secluded spot in the corner. As he took a sip, the flavor proved disappointingly bland. Lost in thought, he pondered his next course of action.

The CoCID had expressed a desire for substantial information, yet Larry felt that he had very little to go on. It occurred to him that perhaps another round of questioning with Tomas was worth a shot. With his decision made, Larry returned to the interrogation room to find Tomas still seated at the table.

He looked more coherent and awake.

"What's up, Inspector?" Tomas asked. "You need me for more questions?"

Larry nodded. "Yeah, just a few more."

"Great, I'll do my best," Tomas replied.

Larry leaned in, focusing on gathering any additional details. "Do you recall how long the waitress had been working at the Black Cat? Have you seen her there before?"

"Yeah, I'd seen her around," Tomas replied. "Maybe a few months, not sure."

Larry pressed further, hoping to uncover any potential leads. "Where else have you seen her?"

"At the Black Cat, obviously," Tomas replied, looking uncomfortable.

Larry noticed Tomas' discomfort and changed tack. "Are you okay?"

"Yeah, I'm good," Tomas assured him.

Larry made a swift decision, reaching into his pocket to retrieve the key. He unlocked the handcuffs that restrained Tomas' hands, surprising him.

"What's going on?" Tomas asked, perplexed.

"You're free to go," Larry declared. "But remember, if you recall anything, you must contact us immediately. Understood?"

Tomas nodded, rubbing his wrists. "Got it."

As Tomas left the room, Larry sighed heavily, sinking back into the chair. However, his brief respite was interrupted by a knock at the door.

"Come in," Larry called out.

"Hey, Inspector," Gwen said as she entered.

"Have you found something, Gwen?" Larry asked, a glimmer of hope in his eyes.

"I have," Gwen confirmed. "The Black Cat is more than it seems. I can't say for sure what's going on, but I witnessed some peculiar things."

Larry leaned forward, eager to hear the details. "Like what?"

Gwen's expression grew solemn. "I saw the bartender carrying a body bag out of the back of the bar."

"Similar to the one Tomas had?" Larry inquired.

"I'm not entirely sure," Gwen admitted. "It was dark, and I couldn't see the contents clearly. It could have been anything."

Larry absorbed the information, mentally connecting the dots. "What else?"

"I noticed some longshoremen entering the bar as well. There were quite a few people inside," Gwen revealed.

"Did they spot you?" Larry asked, concerned about Gwen's safety.

"I don't think so," Gwen assured him. "I was across the street."

Larry nodded, appreciating her caution. "Anything else?"

"That's all I witnessed, sir," Gwen replied. "I briefed Alan about what to look out for."

"Gwen, you did a great job," Larry acknowledged.

"Thank you, sir," Gwen responded earnestly.

"See you later," Larry said, offering her a nod of gratitude.

Gwen left the interrogation room, closing the door behind her with a clang.

Larry called out to the guard stationed outside the door.

"Guard! Open the door, please."

¤

Larry returned to the squad room, spotting Horace stationed at his desk. Horace looked up, acknowledging Larry's presence.

"Hey, boss," Horace greeted him.

Larry approached the desk, a sense of urgency in his voice. "I need you to do something for me."

Curiosity piqued, Horace leaned in. "Okay, what is it?"

"I need you to stay here and hold down the fort," Larry instructed. "If Alan returns, just tell him that I've gone out."

Horace raised an eyebrow. "Where are you headed?"

"I need to locate him. He took over from Gwen on the Black Cat stakeout, and I suspect he may have landed himself in some sort of trouble."

Horace nodded. "Consider it done. I'll make sure to pass on the message."

"Thank you, Horace," Larry expressed his gratitude.

Without wasting any time, Larry headed towards the exit, determined to find Alan and ensure his safety.

Chapter 6

Larry hurried along the street, making his way towards the Black Cat. Concern for Alan weighed heavily on his mind. Alan was not accustomed to fieldwork, but with a small team, everyone had to take their turn on stakeouts. Larry worried about Alan's eagerness and potential vulnerability in a challenging situation. He hoped that Alan hadn't gotten himself into trouble.

As Larry entered the dimly lit bar, the lively atmosphere engulfed him. Conversations filled the air, accompanied by the clinking of glasses.

Larry's presence garnered a few glances from the patrons, but they quickly returned to their conversations. He approached the bar and settled onto one of the stools. The bartender, a large bald man with a goatee, approached him.

"What can I get you?" the bartender asked.

"Give me a double shoggoth straight," Larry requested, his weariness evident.

"Rough night?" the bartender inquired, pouring the drink.

"And it's only four o'clock," Larry replied with a hint of resignation.

The bartender placed a glass of thick, black liquid in front of Larry, who wasted no time in downing the foul-tasting drink. Taking a quick survey of the bar, Larry noticed a large man sitting alone in the corner, his gaze fixed on him. Another shabbily dressed man entered the bar, trying to blend in or avoid eye contact with anyone.

Larry's eyes scanned the room, searching for Alan, but he couldn't spot him. The bartender leaned closer, offering a piece of information.

"If you're looking for the cop," the bartender whispered, "he's in the basement."

Confused, Larry asked, "What cop?"

"The guy who came in earlier. He asked me to watch out for his friend, saying he might show up. Then, about ten minutes ago, he went down to the basement."

"An older guy in the gray suit?" Larry clarified.

"Yeah, that's him," the bartender confirmed.

Appreciative of the tip, Larry left the stool and made his way towards the basement door. Descending the stairs, he reached a locked wooden door with a sign that read "Supplies." Knocking yielded no response, but sounds of distress emanated from the other side—cries of pain or terror.

Larry's instincts kicked in, and he took a step back before charging at the door, using his shoulder to forcefully crash through it. The room beyond was dimly lit, with only faint light filtering through high, unreachable windows. Larry found himself in a small anteroom connected to a larger space through another door.

In the center of the room, Alan was tied to a chair, and standing menacingly over him was a pale man with long black hair obscuring his eyes. The mysterious figure wore a black leather duster, dark jeans, and boots, and held a silver dagger lightly against Alan's throat.

Reacting swiftly, Larry aimed his gun at the man's head. "Drop the knife," he commanded firmly.

The man complied, letting the knife fall to the floor with a clatter. "I surrender," he declared.

"On your knees, hands on your head!" Larry ordered, his voice laced with authority.

The man knelt down, placing his hands on his head as instructed. Larry swiftly handcuffed him before pushing him against the wall. Finally, he cut Alan free from his restraints.

"Thanks, boss" Alan expressed with relief. "I knew you'd find me."

Larry nodded, a mix of concern and determination in his eyes. "We're not done yet. We need to find out who this guy is and what he wants."

They both shared a sense of renewed purpose as they prepared to uncover the truth behind the events unfolding at the Black Cat.

¤

"What the hell were you doing inside? You were supposed to keep an eye on things from across the street!" Larry exclaimed, his frustration evident.

"I was, but then he came out and went back in again," Alan explained. "I followed him inside, but he made me," Alan replied. "He looked suspicious, so I followed him down here and he caught me."

"What's your name?" Larry said with authority.

"Dornan," the man replied.

As Larry glanced around, he noticed a duffel bag on the floor, alongside a broken jar. Curiosity piqued, he directed his attention towards Dornan.

"What's in the bag, Dornan?" Larry inquired.

"Just supplies," Dornan responded casually.

Alan unzipped the bag, revealing a large stash of cash inside. However, Alan's focus was drawn to the shattered jar.

"What's in the jar?" Alan asked, his tone laced with unease.

"Some people say love is a stronger motivator than money," Dornan cryptically replied.

Intrigued and cautious, Larry walked over to inspect the jar, his eyes widening as he beheld its contents—a woman's severed head.

"Do you have a preference for this type? Blond, tall, skinny, big breasts?" Dornan disturbingly inquired.

Larry's grip tightened around the jar as his shock turned to anger.

"That's my girlfriend, Summer," Dornan said. "I keep her in a jar so we can stay together forever."

Fury surged through Larry as he struggled to process the horrifying revelation. "Where is the rest of Summer?" he demanded, his voice trembling with a mix of grief and rage.

"It's a long story," Dornan reluctantly replied.

"We've got nothing but time," Larry declared firmly, determined to uncover the truth.

Dornan hesitated before finally speaking. "Do you know about sloths?" he asked.

"The slow, cute animals?" Alan responded, somewhat bewildered.

"Yes, exactly. I used to have a pet sloth until a hunter killed it for a bounty," Dornan explained, his voice tinged with bitterness.

"I remember those bounties," Larry mentioned. "My Dad used to hunt them."

"And that's why he was a heartless idiot," Dornan asserted. "That sloth never harmed anyone. So, I killed the hunter, skinned him, and took his place."

Shocked by the revelation, Larry stared at Dornan, struggling to comprehend his macabre actions. "When did this happen?" he inquired, his voice filled with disbelief.

"A few months ago," Dornan answered matter-of-factly.

Larry's gaze intensified, his eyes locked on Dornan's. "And where did this happen?" he pressed.

"Meroe," Dornan revealed.

"Never heard of it," Larry admitted.

"It's an old, abandoned mining colony in Khem," Dornan elaborated. "There used to be a massive iron mine there, but it shut down about twenty years ago when the ore dried up. Now, it's just a forest."

Larry's incredulity lingered as he absorbed the information. "So why were you there?" he inquired, searching for a connection.

"I was tracking a... never mind, it's not important. What matters is, I didn't kill that girl," Dornan confessed, his voice tinged with a mix of guilt and urgency.

"Then who did?" Larry demanded, his tone firm.

Dornan averted his gaze, his expression haunted. "I don't know," he admitted reluctantly.

Larry maintained his unwavering stare. "What were you tracking?" he inquired, hoping for any shred of information.

Dornan looked up at the ceiling, lost in thought, before responding. "A werewolf," he finally revealed.

"Bullshit," Alan interjected, dismissing the notion. "Werewolves are myths."

"I've seen it. I tracked it from Celephais to Sarkomand," Dornan asserted, his conviction unwavering.

Eager to gather more details, Larry pressed further. "Describe it to us. What does this werewolf look like?"

Dornan's voice grew solemn. "He's big, wolf-like, with black fur and red eyes. It's a devil, not a man. I've seen it tear men apart."

Skepticism still lingered in Larry's mind. "How do you know it's a werewolf and not just a peculiar animal?" he questioned, seeking concrete evidence.

Dornan's response came with unwavering certainty. "Because I saw it change forms. It's a werewolf."

Intrigued yet cautious, Larry pushed for more details. "What did it change into? Tell us about its human form."

"It transformed into a man, but not quite. He had pale skin, red eyes, long white hair, and fangs," Dornan explained, his voice laden with a mix of fear and fascination.

Larry's interrogation continued. "What was this man wearing?"

"Nothing," Dornan replied, his tone filled with a sense of dread.

Alan voiced his skepticism once again. "How do you know it was male?"

Dornan's response carried a tinge of uncertainty. "I saw his... well, his private parts. It was pretty impressive."

Alan scoffed at the statement, failing to see its relevance. "And how is that important?"

"I'm a hunter. I hunt werewolves. I need to know these things," Dornan explained, his voice tinged with a mix of determination and unease.

Eager to piece together the puzzle, Larry inquired further. "So, do you have any leads? Any information that could help us track down this werewolf?"

Dornan nodded, his eyes filled with a mix of determination and fear. "Just that it's male, around six and a half feet tall, with white hair, red eyes, pointed ears, and he wears a leather jacket made from human skin."

Taking in the information, Larry's gaze shifted towards Summer's severed head in the jar.

"I see. And what about Summer here?"

"What about her?"

"She fits that description," Dornan said, his voice heavy with sorrow.

"Yeah, she does," Larry said. He looked at the head in the jar.

"She's a blond and has... blue eyes."

Dornan looked at Larry in disbelief.

"What?"

Larry held up the head in front of him by the hair.

"What about her?"

Dornan's eyes widened as he stared at the head in shock, his previous conviction wavering. "What... what the hell?" he stuttered, recoiling in horror.

Larry's voice carried a mix of accusation and desperation. "Why did you kill her?" he demanded to know, seeking answers.

"I didn't. I swear to God, I didn't kill her," Dornan vehemently denied.

"Then who did?" Larry pressed, his voice filled with determination to uncover the truth.

"It was the werewolf," Dornan confessed, his voice haunted by the weight of his words.

¤

Dornan was escorted to the Police Presidium, where Alan forcefully shoved him into a cell. Frustrated and bewildered, Dornan confronted them, questioning their actions.

"What the hell are you doing?" Dornan protested.

Larry stood firm, his tone resolute. "You will stay here until we figure out what to do with you," he declared.

Dornan's desperation grew. "What are you, new? You can't just throw me in here! I have rights!" he exclaimed.

Larry countered, dismissing his claims. "You have no rights in Dylath-Leen, Dornan. We'll be back later," he stated coldly.

Dornan's pleas continued, pleading for their reconsideration. "Bullshit! Come on, you can't just leave me here!" he pleaded desperately.

Larry closed the cell door, leaving Dornan locked inside. He turned to Alan, ready to discuss their next course of action.

"I think he saw a Ravager and went insane. He's been hunting Ravagers, and his imagination embellished the story," Alan speculated.

Larry remained steadfast in his conviction. "And he's not our guy," he asserted with confidence.

"I agree," Alan concurred. "He's not our guy."

Larry offered a suggestion, aware of the need for rest. "You should go home, get some rest. We can interrogate him again in the morning," he proposed.

"Thanks, boss," Alan acknowledged, accepting the advice. "See you tomorrow."

With that, Alan exited the building, leaving Larry to follow a few minutes later. Larry made his way back to his apartment, his mind still occupied with the troubling events that had unfolded.

¤

The dimly lit room was filled with a tense atmosphere as Larry sat across from Dani at their small dinner table. They tried to have dinner together every evening, a momentary respite from the constant surveillance and strict rules that governed their lives.

Larry glanced at Dani, noticing the conflicted expression on her face. He could tell something was bothering her, and as a father, he wanted to provide her with guidance and support, even in this constrained environment. He cleared his throat and spoke gently, "Dani, you seem a bit troubled. Is there something on your mind?"

Dani hesitated for a moment, unsure whether she should voice her concerns. She knew the Schola, the secretive institution she attended, instilled a sense of loyalty to the Overlords in the tyros, but she couldn't help but feel a growing dissatisfaction within her. She finally mustered the courage to speak, her voice trembling slightly, "Dad, it's just... I feel like I'm losing myself at the Schola. We're taught to be loyal servants of the Overlords, but I don't know if that's who I really am."

Larry's expression softened, realizing the weight of her words. He knew how difficult it was for Dani to question the system they lived in, and he admired her strength for doing so. He reached across the table and gently placed his hand on hers, offering comfort. "Dani, it's natural for teenagers to question and explore their identities. I understand the pressure you feel at the Schola, but remember, you are your own person."

Dani looked into her father's eyes, finding solace in his words. "But what if they find out, Dad? What if they punish me for not conforming?"

Larry sighed, fully aware of the risks involved. He leaned closer, his voice barely above a whisper. "Dani, I won't lie to you. Going against the expectations of the Overlords carries risks. But I want you to know that your happiness and well-being are important to me. We'll face any challenges together, as a family."

Dani's eyes glistened with gratitude and relief. She squeezed her father's hand, feeling a sense of unity and strength emanating from their connection. "Thanks, Dad. I don't know what I'd do without you."

Larry's heart ached as he looked at Dani, seeing a glimmer of his wife, Charlotte, in her eyes. It had been eight long years since the Overlords had taken Charlotte away, and the pain of her absence still lingered in their lives. He held back his own emotions, wanting to be a pillar of strength for his daughter.

A pang of sorrow passed through Larry's thoughts as he remembered the day Charlotte disappeared, leaving behind unanswered questions and a void that seemed impossible to fill. He silently vowed to protect Dani at all costs, to shield her from the same fate that had befallen her mother.

Larry squeezed Dani's hand gently, finding solace in their shared connection. "I miss your mother every day, Dani," he admitted softly. "But I won't let the same fate befall you. We'll find a way to navigate through this, to keep our family intact."

Dani nodded, tears welling up in her eyes. She understood the pain her father carried, and she admired his strength and determination. "I miss Mom too, Dad," she whispered. "But we'll face the challenges together, just like you said."

Larry managed a small smile, his heart swelling with love and pride for his daughter. In Dani, he saw a spark of resilience and defiance that gave him hope. He knew that together, they could weather any storm, honor Charlotte's memory, and fight for a future where freedom and happiness prevailed.

As they finished their meal, Larry and Dani shared a moment of silence, their thoughts filled with unspoken words and the weight of their shared burdens.

Chapter 7

"Good morning, team. Anything new to report?" Larry asked as he entered the squad room the next morning.

"Sir, we have a new one," Alan responded.

"Another killing?" Larry inquired.

"No, a kidnapping," Gwen chimed in.

"Damn it, who was it this time?" Larry questioned, concern etching his face.

"A man named O'Neill, sir. He has a wife and three kids," Gwen informed.

Larry's curiosity grew, and he questioned further, "Then why is it assigned to us and not Missing Persons?"

"I don't know, sir. The CoCID just said to give you the file when you came in," Alan said.

Larry pressed for more details, "What do we know about him?"

"He was a mid-level trader, sir. Doing pretty well, but not enough to make him a target. His kids said he left for a meeting and never came back," Gwen explained.

Confused about the connection to their murder victims, Larry sought clarification, "What does this have to do with our murder victims?"

"Nothing, sir," Gwen replied nonchalantly.

Larry took the file and retreated to his office, eager to gather more information. As he delved into the report, he discovered that a man named O'Neill, aged 50, had gone missing two days ago. The details provided no leads; the man had simply vanished. Larry pondered whether it was the act of a solitary individual nursing a grudge or one of the many factions that held grievances against the government. Regardless, it wasn't a murder case falling under his jurisdiction.

He carried the file to the office of the CoCID and knocked on the door.

"Come in," he heard her shout.

Larry entered the room and found Superintendent Gaunt sitting at her desk, holding a red folder. She gestured for him to take a seat in front of her.

Larry complied, settling into the chair and waiting for her to speak. The CoCID opened the folder, revealing several photographs, which she spread out before him.

"What do you see?" she asked, her tone expectant.

Leaning forward, Larry scrutinized the pictures. After a moment, he responded, "I see seven identical women, including two of our victims."

"Go on," the CoCID prompted.

"The women are all young, in their mid-twenties, and they appear to be related. The resemblance is undeniable," Larry observed.

"Good, what else?" she prodded.

"I don't see anything else, CoCID," Larry confessed, unsure of what he might be missing.

"Look again," she insisted, her annoyance evident.

Larry scrutinized the pictures once more, his gaze focused. And then it hit him.

"The room," Larry stated, a realization dawning upon him.

"Go on," the CoCID urged, her eyes fixed on him.

"They are all on a lab table," Larry concluded.

"They were, before they escaped," the CoCID confirmed.

"Escaped?" Larry echoed, surprised by the revelation.

The CoCID stared at him, waiting for Larry to draw the correct conclusion.

"Our murder victim clones escaped from a laboratory, and now someone is killing them to cover it up," Larry deduced, a mix of astonishment and concern coloring his voice.

"Exactly," the CoCID affirmed.

"Why would anyone do that?" Larry pondered, the question lingering in his mind.

"We don't know yet. But I need you to find out," the CoCID instructed, her tone conveying the urgency of the matter.

"My team is already working on it," Larry assured her.

"Good, keep me posted," the CoCID replied, signifying the importance of regular updates.

"Yes, CoCID," Larry acknowledged respectfully, rising from his seat and making his way back to his office.

In the hallway, he found his team gathered around a large table, engrossed in their work.

"What's up?" Larry inquired, joining them.

"We were just about to come find you," Gwen replied.

"We're going through the victims' personal effects," Horace added, pointing to the items spread out on the table.

Larry approached the table and examined the belongings. Among them were a book of poetry, a photograph of a middle-aged man in a soldier's uniform, a handful of love letters, a pack of cigarettes, and a prescription bottle containing pills.

Larry's attention was drawn to the pill bottle, and he read the label aloud, "100MG CLONAZEPAM, TAKE ONE EVERY SIX TO EIGHT HOURS AS NEEDED FOR ANXIETY."

Horace provided his observation, "This victim was a drug addict."

Larry considered the information but couldn't shake off the connection. "No, our murder victims are clones that escaped from a laboratory. This must be related to that. Gwen, find out what this medication is used for."

"Yes, sir," Gwen acknowledged, her focus shifting to the new task.

Larry then inquired about the Medical Examiner's report on the victims, which Gwen promptly handed to him.

"Thank you, Gwen," Larry said, determined to uncover more clues in their quest for the truth.

¤

Larry quickly skimmed through the report, reaffirming what he already knew—the victims had died from exsanguination caused by multiple stab wounds.

As he delved into the details, the CoCID approached him, her presence commanding his attention. She inquired, "Anything interesting?"

Larry held up the first report. "The first one, Susan Jones, was stabbed six times with a long sharp instrument, likely a sword. It resulted in severe internal injuries."

The CoCID nodded, recalling the case. "Yes, I remember that. She was also bitten, correct?"

"Yes, CoCID," Larry confirmed, "but that was likely the work of vermin post-mortem."

Moving on to the next report, Larry continued, "The second victim, from Leen, has been identified as Alison Craven."

Curiosity piqued, the CoCID inquired, "What do we know about her?"

"Not much," Larry admitted, "She was never reported missing."

Taking the reports from Larry, the CoCID read through them herself. Her eyes narrowed as she reached the end of Alison's report. Something caught her attention.

"What is it?" Larry asked, noticing her pause.

Her voice carried a hint of intrigue as she responded, "Her brother, William Craven, was reported missing in action a few years ago. He's presumed dead."

Surprised, Larry questioned, "How do you know that, CoCID?"

"I remember it because it was one of the cases I worked on when I first arrived here," she explained. "We had no leads at the time, and his body was never found."

Larry picked up a photograph he found among Alison's belongings and handed it to the CoCID. "This photo was discovered among Alison's possessions. It shows a soldier. Perhaps it's William Craven?"

The CoCID took the photo, inspecting it.

"How does Alison have a brother? She wasn't the original."

"We can only speculate," she said. "Please, continue with the reports."

Larry summarized the remaining reports, but there was nothing of significant interest within them.

The CoCID placed the reports in her briefcase, indicating that she would review them later. However, she had another matter to discuss.

"There is something else I need to address," the CoCID began, taking a deep breath. She glanced around, ensuring privacy.

"I have decided to promote you to Special Class," she announced, her voice filled with gravity. "This comes with a pay raise and added benefits, such as your own reserved parking space here at the Police Presidium. It will also grant you access to certain Overlord records. However, it will put you under Overlord scrutiny."

Larry absorbed the weight of the decision and responded earnestly, "I understand, CoCID."

"It was not a decision I made lightly," the CoCID reassured him.

"Thank you, CoCID," Larry expressed his gratitude.

"You're welcome, Inspector," the CoCID said. "Now, you're dismissed."

Acknowledging the end of the conversation, Larry replied, "Yes, CoCID."

With that, Larry went to his office, his mind filled with a mix of anticipation and the weight of his new responsibilities as he ventured into the realm of the Special Class.

¤

Larry returned to his desk, finding a skinny kid in a red hoodie sitting in his chair, engrossed in his phone. Recognizing him as Matt, an acquaintance of Dani's, Larry greeted him, "Hello, Matt."

Matt looked up and replied, "Hello, sir."

"Shouldn't you be at the Schola now?" Larry asked. "What can I do for you?"

Matt hesitated before speaking, "I, uh, I wanted to see if you could help me find a job or something."

Larry took a moment to consider the request. "Doing what?"

"It doesn't matter," Matt said. "I just need something. I'm trying to save up enough money to get a place of my own."

Larry understood the desire for independence and self-sufficiency. "Matt, the Schola will provide for you until your graduation."

"Yeah, I know," Matt replied. "But I need to do this on my own. You understand, right?"

Sighing, Larry nodded. "I get it, kid. You want to pave your own path and not rely solely on the Schola."

Matt clarified, "I have to stay in school. It's mandatory. I have to. But I want to live somewhere else. And to do that, I need a job."

Larry weighed the options and cautioned, "Matt, I can't find you a job."

"Please, sir," Matt pleaded. "I need to try."

Concerned for Matt's well-being, Larry spoke with honesty, "If you leave the Schola without authorization, you'll be hunted down and face severe consequences. Military penal battalion or even the Culling. Is that what you want?"

Matt shook his head, fear evident in his eyes. "No, sir."

"Then go back to the Schola and keep a low profile," Larry advised firmly.

"Yes, sir," Matt replied, disappointment coloring his voice. He stood up and left the office. Larry sighed and locked the door.

Feeling the weight of the situation, Larry picked up the phone and dialed a number. After a few rings, a voice answered, "Hello?"

"Crawford, it's Nodens," Larry identified himself. "I have something for you."

Curious, Crawford asked, "What have you got?"

"Investigate a tyro named Matt Caulfield," Larry instructed.

"Why?" Crawford inquired.

"He expressed a desire to leave the Schola," Larry explained. "I'm not sure if he's a potential shadow, but if he is, he might lead you to a nest of radicals."

"I'll look into it immediately," Crawford responded. "Thanks."

"Of course," Larry acknowledged before ending the call.

Larry couldn't help but think about the stark differences between the training and future prospects for girls versus boys at the Schola. The boys' experiences, like everything else about the Schola, were shrouded in secrecy, unspoken and absent from any history lessons. However, Larry knew that the ceremony held at the school was of great significance. Every tyro was required to attend, ensuring that the government could maintain strict oversight and prevent any escape from the watchful eye of the Overlords.

Sitting back in his chair, Larry contemplated Matt's fate. He hoped that Matt wouldn't attempt to leave. The consequences for defying the Overlords were severe. They didn't tolerate such acts of rebellion, often purging those who dared to challenge their authority, sometimes even targeting those who didn't.

Chapter 8

Larry grabbed a tray of food from the cafeteria, though he despised the taste of the spicy powder that was meant to improve the flavor. Despite his distaste, he had no choice but to eat it since it was the only option available. Finding an empty table, he sat down alone to have his meal.

As he sat there, a woman with long brown hair and dressed in a white and red dress approached and smiled at him. Larry nodded in acknowledgment.

"Hey," she greeted him.

"Hello," he replied.

"I'm Kary," she introduced herself.

"Nodens," Larry responded.

Kary asked, "Do you mind if I sit here?"

"Go ahead," Larry replied, gesturing for her to take a seat.

She placed her tray on the table and sat down, prompting Larry to stare at her for a moment.

"What?" she asked, furrowing her brow.

"You look familiar. Have we met before?" Larry inquired.

"I don't think so," Kary replied with a smile "I would have remembered you.

Larry tilted his head, trying to recall where he might have seen her.

"You do look familiar, though," she continued.

"I'm Nodens," Larry said, hoping it would trigger a memory.

Kary smiled and nodded. "Yeah, I know."

Curiosity piqued, Larry asked, "I'm an Inspector. What do you do here at the Police Presidium?"

"I'm a telepath," Kary revealed. "Well, still in training. I haven't been out in the field yet."

Larry raised an eyebrow. "Have you gotten to meet anyone interesting?"

"A few. What about you?" Kary inquired.

"I meet interesting people all the time. Most of them are dead," Larry replied, his tone tinged with a hint of weariness.

Suddenly, a man in a dark gray suit approached their table. Kary immediately straightened up and greeted him warmly.

"Hello, sir," she said.

The man wore a tired expression and carried a file under his arm. He acknowledged Kary before turning his attention to Larry.

"I'm Commissar Miller from Internal Affairs," Miller said.

"I'm Inspector Nodens," Larry introduced himself.

Miller's frown deepened slightly. He sat down next to him without asking permission and opened his file.

"I need to ask you a few questions," Miller stated.

Larry was taken aback by Miller's directness. "About what?"

Miller selected a photo from the file, revealing a bloody dead body.

"He was found like this. We need to know who he is," Miller explained.

Kary gave Larry a strange look as he examined the photograph. A sense of unease settled within him, signaling that something was amiss.

"Do you recognize him?" Miller pressed for an answer.

Larry studied the image once more. The man depicted was middle-aged, with a goatee and thinning hair. He seemed vaguely familiar.

"I believe this man's name is O'Neill. He was reported missing a few days ago, and the case was assigned to my team," Larry responded.

Miller's gaze sharpened, his tone accusatory. "So, you're saying you know this man?"

"I've never met him. I just read the case file," Larry clarified.

Miller's demeanor grew more intense. "We can do this in one of two ways, Inspector. You can be cooperative, or I can make it unpleasant. The choice is yours."

Perplexed, Larry asked, "What are you implying, Commissar?"

"You've been identified at the scene of a crime," Miller stated bluntly.

"Where and when?" Larry inquired, his confusion mounting.

"Approximately thirty minutes ago, you were seen fleeing a warehouse," Miller revealed.

Larry's brow furrowed. "I was?"

"Yes," Miller affirmed.

"Thirty minutes ago, I was in a meeting with the Commander of Criminal Investigations," Larry countered, his voice steady.

Miller observed Larry silently for a moment before sighing. "Is that so?"

"Yes. She can confirm it," Larry asserted.

Miller's gaze held steady as he weighed his options. Eventually, he closed his file.

Miller conceded. "You can go."

"Actually, I was here first. You go," Larry suggested, his tone implying a desire to end the encounter.

Larry watched as Miller stood up, a hint of tension lingering in the air.

Miller frowned, clearly displeased, and walked away, leaving Larry to contemplate the strange turn of events. He refocused his attention on his tray of food.

"Okay, Kary. What did you gather from that conversation?" Larry asked, his curiosity piqued.

Kary shifted uncomfortably and replied, "Nothing. I didn't really have a chance to read you."

Larry studied Kary intently, sensing there was more to her than met the eye. He nodded in understanding.

"You know Miller?" he inquired.

"Yeah," Kary responded. "I know him." Her expression tightened with concern. "We should go."

"Go where?" Larry questioned, uncertain about the sudden urgency.

"Anywhere. If they know I'm talking with you, they'll be watching. We should find somewhere else to talk," Kary suggested urgently.

"Okay," Larry agreed, recognizing the need for caution.

¤

Kary hastily finished her meal, and together they made their way out of the cafeteria into a sprawling hallway. Kary appeared anxious, glancing around nervously.

"Where exactly are we supposed to be going?" she asked, her voice filled with unease.

Larry raised an eyebrow, and Kary let out a nervous laugh.

"Sorry," she apologized. "I can't say anything here. Let's just go."

"Come with me," Larry offered, leading her towards the parking garage. They both entered the Shantak and Larry locked the doors before turning to Kary.

"Now, what is all this about?" he demanded.

Kary looked at him with a mixture of fear and hesitation.

"I can't tell you," she replied quietly.

Larry's frustration grew. "Kary, you pulled me away to say something you won't even disclose? Is it classified, or do you simply not trust me?"

Kary's gaze faltered, but she ultimately made up her mind. She locked eyes with Larry.

"I trust you," she confessed.

"In that case, what is it?" Larry pressed.

"It's about Commissar Miller," Kary revealed.

"What about him?" Larry inquired, curious yet cautious.

"He's not... well, he's not a good person," Kary admitted, her voice tinged with apprehension.

"I've heard rumors," Larry acknowledged.

Kary nodded vigorously. "Rumors don't do him justice. He's... he's done terrible things, far beyond the usual misconduct of the police. I mean truly awful."

"Like what?" Larry probed, his interest piqued.

"He resorts to brutal methods to extract confessions," Kary disclosed.

"I've done the same on occasion," Larry admitted with a hint of regret.

"He has also framed at least three innocent individuals that I'm aware of," Kary continued, her voice filled with disgust.

"Unfortunately, such acts are not uncommon under the Overlords' reign," Larry remarked with a tinge of bitterness.

"I know, but this goes beyond that. The victims merely angered him by standing up to him," Kary explained.

"I've witnessed people being killed for far less," Larry remarked grimly.

"But don't just take my word for it. Investigate it yourself," Kary urged.

She reached into her pocket and retrieved her cell phone.

"Here. It contains all the information I have, along with the password to access my files. However, please refrain from looking into anything else. My personal profile is private," Kary cautioned.

"Sure," Larry agreed, accepting her phone and briefly glancing at it. "Thanks. I'll see what I can find."

"Thank you, Nodens," Kary expressed her gratitude, leaning over to kiss him on the cheek.

"Kary?" Larry called out, prompting her to look at him.

"I apologize for doubting you," he said sincerely.

A warm smile crossed Kary's face, and she kissed his cheek once again.

"Did you manage to read me?" Larry inquired.

"Oh!" Kary exclaimed, her smile widening. "Yes, I did."

She extended her hand, and Larry placed his own hand on top of hers. She pressed down on it gently and then released it.

"I hope your report reflects my cooperation," Larry remarked.

Kary beamed with reassurance. "Don't worry," she assured him. "I'll make sure it portrays everything accurately."

Larry nodded, watching as Kary exited the car and headed towards the elevators.

"You forgot your phone!" he called out.

"Oh, right!" Kary exclaimed, quickly returning to retrieve her phone from Larry's hand.

"Thanks." She smiled before turning and resuming her path towards the elevators. Larry watched her departure, letting out a sigh before making his way back to the squad room.

Chapter 9

Larry returned to his office and settled in. As he checked his inbox, he noticed a flashing message that caught his attention. Opening it, he discovered his new Special Class identification code. Without hesitation, he entered the code and initiated a search for records pertaining to an Overlord genetic experiment.

The search yielded an overwhelming number of results, so Larry refined it, focusing on experiments involving young women. The list narrowed down to a more manageable one hundred thirty files. Determined to find specific information about Claire Noble or Alison Craven, Larry delved into those remaining files.

Among the documents, he discovered an entry for Claire Noble. Larry carefully examined the contents of the file.

Her file revealed a heartbreaking story. She had been a victim of sexual assault and subsequently struggled with substance abuse. However, after undergoing rehabilitation and therapy, she was reunited with her daughter, who had been placed in foster care. Alison found work at a fast-food restaurant and resided in a modest apartment with her child.

Intrigued by the discrepancies between the official file and the truth, Larry entered the override code, 5366, to access the actual report. The screen transformed, displaying the genuine account of Claire Noble's ordeal.

Claire had also been a victim of sexual assault, but her fate took a darker turn. The Overlords had abducted her and subjected her to genetic experimentation. Using her DNA, they created six identical clones. All seven women, including Claire, were subjected to extensive tests that altered their memories and personalities. While they believed they had participated in a study on learning and memory, their memories were fabricated, but the physiological changes in their brains were genuine. After thirty days, the women had their memories altered once more, this time implanting more positive experiences. They were then released into society, each with a new identity.

Larry reviewed the information regarding the other six clones, contemplating the implications of their existence:

Clone 1, Jennifer Allen, had become a teacher.
Clone 2, Heather Jensen, pursued a career in medicine as a doctor.
Clone 3, Alison Craven, took on the role of an accountant.
Clone 4, Lisa Taylor, became a police officer.
Clone 5, Karen Stone, found her passion as a cook.
Clone 6, Susan Jones, pursued a career as a singer.

Recognizing the potential danger and significance of this information, Larry swiftly sent the list of names to the patrol unit, instructing them to be on the lookout for any individuals matching the descriptions. However, before he could fully process the situation, his phone suddenly rang, demanding his attention. Glancing at the screen, he discovered that one of the individuals on the list, a woman bearing a striking resemblance to Alison Craven, had just entered a nearby coffee shop.

Without hesitation, Larry quickly sent instructions to bring the woman to the Police Presidium, realizing that they were one step closer to uncovering the truth behind the Overlords' disturbing experiment.

¤

She appeared visibly uneasy in her surroundings, her expression reflecting her discomfort.

"Give me a report, Sergeant," Larry demanded.

"Sir, during our routine patrol, we encountered a woman who bore a striking resemblance to the circulated picture of Alison Craven," the Sergeant began. "We approached her and asked her to come with us, and she agreed. Initially, nothing seemed suspicious, but when we ran her ID, it turned out to be Alison Craven."

Larry turned to the woman and asked, "Are you Alison Craven?"

The woman seemed taken aback that they knew her name. "Yes... Yes, I am Alison Craven. But how did you...?"

Larry retrieved his phone and showed her a picture of her with a baby. "We have another Alison Craven here... in the morgue. She looks exactly like you. Can you explain this?"

The woman's hands flew to cover her mouth in shock. "Oh my God... Oh my God..." she muttered, tears streaming down her face. "I had a sister... I had a sister..." Her body trembled as she sobbed, and Larry gently took hold of her arm to offer comfort.

"There is also another woman who closely resembles you. Her name was Claire Noble," Larry continued, his voice filled with sympathy.

Still crying, the woman nodded. "Claire... Claire had been in rehab for two years. She was released a year ago, and then..."

Larry interrupted, pressing for more information. "How do you know her?"

"We... we were identical twins," she stammered. "She was released by the Overlords as a control subject. They told me they would release her after the experiment was over. I... I didn't think they would kill her..."

"You are actually one of seven. Two of them have been murdered, along with another woman who bears a resemblance to you but was not part of the experiment," Larry revealed, his tone grave.

"They told me I was the only one. They lied to me. They told me our parents were dead," she whispered, her voice filled with anguish.

"That will be all, Sergeant," Larry dismissed the officer, who promptly exited the room.

Now alone with the woman, Larry faced her directly. "So, you believed that you and Claire were identical twins. You were unaware of any others."

She nodded, tears still streaming down her face. "I had heard rumors of seven identical girls, but I never believed it. I was too preoccupied with my own life, and my sister seemed to be doing the same."

"We suspect that someone connected to the experiment is targeting the seven of you. Do you have any thoughts on who that might be?" Larry inquired, his eyes fixed on her.

After a moment of contemplation, she responded, "There were rumors suggesting that one of the seven might be a traitor, but I don't know anything more than that."

Before she could elaborate further, a beeping sound emanated from Larry's pocket, drawing his attention. Retrieving his phone, he saw a message from Horace.

"We found another one."

The message was accompanied by an address. Larry swiftly made his decision.

"Miss Craven, I'd like you to stay here for the time being, for your own safety. We will arrange for security at your home," Larry instructed, concern evident on his face. "I must leave now."

He swiftly exited the room and made his way to his car, ready to respond to the new lead provided by Horace, determined to uncover the truth and protect the remaining individuals involved in the sinister experiment.

¤

Larry arrived at the provided address, situated in the Old Dylath District. As he entered the house, he noticed three officers standing in the foyer, their attention focused on a lifeless body. Larry immediately recognized the face and attire—it was Jennifer Allen, clone number two.

Approaching the body, Larry observed a deep gash on the neck, with blood forming a small pool beneath it. The expression on Jennifer's face revealed shock, and her eyes remained wide open, evidence that she had come face-to-face with her killer.

Larry scanned the room and noticed an open window on the first floor. He swiftly commanded, "Sergeant, seal off the entire area. No one enters or exits until further notice."

Entering the room, Larry crouched next to the body, examining the pool of blood near the neck. The cut appeared rough and jagged, unlike the clean wounds inflicted on previous victims.

"Our killer has adjusted his approach. The smoother wounds we saw before were likely the work of a ravager. This time, he targeted the neck instead of the torso," Larry deduced.

Horace joined him, assessing the scene. "Looks like you were right, Boss. We need to catch this person before they strike again."

"I've secured the area, but the perpetrator is likely long gone by now. Instruct the patrol to thoroughly search the building and neighborhood. We need to find any potential witnesses," Larry instructed.

"Yes, sir," Horace acknowledged, and the officers swiftly began their tasks.

Larry rose from the body, glancing out the window once more. His gaze fell upon a fire escape on the opposite side.

"Scan the fire escape for DNA evidence," Larry ordered, aware that it was a slim chance but worth pursuing.

An officer promptly approached the fire escape and conducted the scan. After a brief moment, he reported, "The fire escape is clean, sir."

"I suspected as much," Larry murmured.

"I found this on the victim," Horace informed him.

Inspecting further, Larry noticed a small pill bottle, which he opened to reveal three pills inside.

"Check if these match the ones we found with Claire Noble," Larry directed one of the officers.

The officer read the label on the bottle and responded, "Filled by a Dr. Llanfer at The Facility."

Larry frowned, a sense of unease settling within him. "Horace, it seems we need to have a conversation with this Dr. Llanfer."

The two of them left the house and made their way back to the Shantak, embarking on a silent drive toward The Facility, their determination unwavering as they sought answers and pursued justice.

Chapter 10

Ten minutes later, Larry pulled into the parking lot of The Facility. He retrieved the pill bottle from his pocket and joined Horace in stepping out of the car. They found themselves facing a tall, immaculate building adorned with the sign "Welcome to The Facility."

As they entered, they approached a large desk where a beautiful blonde woman sat. She greeted them with a friendly smile, asking, "How may I help you?"

Larry introduced themselves, stating, "Inspector Nodens and Sergeant Whately. CID."

The woman nodded, reaching for the phone on her desk. After a brief conversation, she informed them, "They're on their way down."

Curiosity piqued, Larry inquired, "Who?"

She responded, "Who do you think? Dr. Llanfer and Jennifer, of course."

Larry took a seat while waiting, and within a minute, a man and a woman emerged from an elevator. The woman bore an uncanny resemblance to the receptionist at the desk, while the man wore a neat suit and tie, with well-groomed hair and a clean-shaven face. Larry and Horace stood up as they approached.

Addressing the man, Larry asked, "Dr. Llanfer?"

The man nodded in acknowledgment.

"I'm Inspector Nodens, and this is my associate, Sergeant Whately. We would like to ask you a few questions."

Dr. Llanfer fell silent for a moment before agreeing, "Yes, of course."

Larry gestured toward privacy, asking, "Is there somewhere we can speak in private?"

Dr. Llanfer led them to his office, where he took a seat at his desk. Larry settled into an adjacent chair, while Horace positioned himself behind his inspector.

Curiosity driving the conversation forward, Larry began by inquiring, "What is your role here, Doctor?"

"I'm a chemist. I develop new medical compounds for the company," Dr. Llanfer explained.

Larry nodded, retrieving the pill bottle from his pocket and sliding it across the desk. "Do you recognize this?"

Dr. Llanfer examined the bottle and confirmed, "Yes, that's a sample of the drug I developed for our clients. It's one of the many drugs we've created here."

Seeking further information, Larry probed, "And what is the purpose of this drug?"

"It's designed to enhance intelligence," Dr. Llanfer replied.

Larry's curiosity deepened as he pressed, "Who are your clients?"

"I'm sorry, but I'm not at liberty to disclose their identities," Dr. Llanfer replied.

Larry's tone grew more serious as he pointed out, "We have found three deceased women in possession of this drug. Can you explain that?"

Dr. Llanfer faltered, stating, "I can't."

Larry stared at him in silence, then motioned for Horace to retrieve a notepad and pen. As Horace complied, Larry fixed his gaze on Dr. Llanfer. "Tell me, does this drug have any connection to clones?"

Confusion clouded Dr. Llanfer's expression. "Clones?"

"Yes," Larry affirmed.

Dr. Llanfer hesitated before responding, "No, it has nothing to do with clones."

Larry's confusion mirrored Dr. Llanfer's as he sought clarification. "But the victims we've discovered, as well as your receptionist and secretary, are clones. Can you explain that?"

Dr. Llanfer appeared startled, struggling to respond. "I... I can't."

"Why not?" Larry pressed.

"I genuinely don't know anything about it," Dr. Llanfer insisted.

Larry nodded pensively before posing another question. "How long have Jennifer and...?"

Dr. Llanfer interrupted, clarifying, "They aren't clones. They are grown in labs."

Larry's confusion deepened, and he probed further. "So, their eggs were harvested or something?"

Dr. Llanfer hesitated briefly before confirming, "Yes, that's precisely what I mean."

Seizing the opportunity for more information, Larry asked, "And where are these eggs grown?"

"I don't know," Dr. Llanfer admitted.

"You're lying! Are they grown here?" Larry pressed, his voice growing stern.

"I genuinely don't know!" Dr. Llanfer insisted, his sweating intensifying.

Larry contemplated the situation and continued his line of questioning. "Who is the mother of these eggs?"

"I don't know! I swear to God, I don't know anything!" Dr. Llanfer pleaded.

After a moment of silence, Larry inquired, "What happens to these... specimens?"

"They are grown and then shipped off to be sold," Dr. Llanfer confessed, avoiding eye contact.

Perplexed, Larry sought further clarification. "What do you mean by 'sold'?"

Dr. Llanfer glanced away uncomfortably. "Some... some of them are sold as slaves. Others are used for..."

He trailed off, leaving Larry with a raised eyebrow. "Used for what?"

"S-s-snuff films. Some of them are used in snuff films," Dr. Llanfer reluctantly admitted.

Larry maintained his composed demeanor as he questioned, "How do you know this?"

Dr. Llanfer paused, averting his gaze. "I... I've heard about it."

"You seem to know a lot about snuff films," Larry commented, suspicion creeping into his tone.

Dr. Llanfer fell silent, refusing to answer.

Larry stood up and nodded to Horace, signaling their departure. "Thank you for your cooperation, Dr. Llanfer. However, we are sealing this facility and taking you and your staff into custody."

Dr. Llanfer protested, "What? Why?"

"You have lied to me, and I can no longer trust you," Larry explained firmly.

"But I haven't lied! I truly don't know anything!" Dr. Llanfer pleaded.

"You haven't told me everything," Larry countered.

Dr. Llanfer remained silent.

Larry turned away, stating, "We're done here. The entire facility will be sealed off until we can unravel what's happening. All staff members will be detained for a comprehensive investigation."

As Larry began walking away, Dr. Llanfer's protests grew desperate. "Hey! You can't do this!"

Larry retorted, "Oh, but I can."

"Please! I need to contact my lawyers!" Dr. Llanfer pleaded.

"It's too late for that. You should have thought about it before lying to me," Larry responded firmly.

"I wasn't lying!" Dr. Llanfer insisted.

Larry stopped momentarily and faced him once more. "One last chance. Tell me the whole truth, or you'll be spending some time in a cell."

"I told you everything I know!" Dr. Llanfer exclaimed, his voice filled with panic.

"You're hiding something," Larry accused.

"I'm not!" Dr. Llanfer protested.

Larry stared at him for a moment, then turned and walked away. Dr. Llanfer's desperate pleas echoed through the hallway as Horace escorted him out of the office.

As Larry disappeared around a corner, the truth remained obscured, and the investigation into The Facility continued, driven by a determination to expose the hidden horrors lurking within.

¤

After a few minutes of walking through the Facility's corridors, Larry entered a lift and pressed the button for the sub-basement. The door shut, and the lift descended smoothly. As the lift came to a stop, Larry stepped out into a dimly lit corridor and turned left. He walked along the corridor for a few meters, finally reaching a large metal door with a battered intercom set into it. The thick glass window on the intercom had multiple cracks running through it, showing signs of previous wear and tear. Larry pressed the button, and the door emitted a buzzing sound as it unlocked. He pushed it open and entered the expansive room beyond.

Inside, Larry found himself standing in the center of a spacious warehouse. The walls were lined with towering shelves that stretched all the way up to the shadowy ceiling. The shelves were filled with neatly arranged boxes, creating a maze-like arrangement within the room. Illuminated by a single overhead light, a table stood in the middle of the warehouse. It displayed an assortment of items, including various knives of different sizes, a loaded 9mm caliber pistol, a length of rope, a hacksaw, a hammer, a screwdriver, a wrench, pliers, and a blowtorch. Larry approached the table, studying the objects before him.

Curiosity piqued, he reached out and picked up the blowtorch, feeling the warmth of the flame against his hand. He inspected it carefully, contemplating its potential uses. Setting it back down, he then took hold of one of the knives, testing its sharpness by lightly running his thumb along the blade. A thin sliver of skin peeled off, dropping onto the table. Satisfied with its sharpness, he placed the knife back down and shifted his attention to the loaded pistol. He picked it up, checked the magazine to ensure it was fully loaded, and placed it back on the table.

With the inventory of items examined, Larry decided to return to the car where Horace was conversing with a group of uniformed officers. Spotting Larry's approach, Horace excused himself from the conversation and walked over to his inspector.

"Sir, we're ready to go whenever you are," Horace informed him.

Larry acknowledged Horace and asked, "Have you found anything, Sergeant?"

Horace shook his head, disappointment evident in his expression. "No, sir."

Larry contemplated for a moment before giving a determined nod. "I want every inch of this place thoroughly searched. We can't afford to miss anything."

Horace responded with a firm salute. "Yes, sir. We'll leave no stone unturned. We'll find something, sir."

"Good," Larry replied. "I'm heading back to the office. Let me know immediately if you discover anything significant."

Horace nodded and replied, "Yes, sir."

With their conversation concluded, Larry turned and made his way back to the car, leaving Horace to coordinate the search efforts. As he entered the vehicle, thoughts raced through his mind, wondering what dark secrets this Facility held and if their search would uncover the truth they were seeking.

Chapter 11

As Larry and Dani sat down for dinner once again, Larry couldn't help but notice the change in Dani's demeanor. Her previously conflicted expression seemed to have transformed into a more determined and positive one, reflecting a heightened devotion to the Overlords. Larry felt a mix of pride and uneasiness in his heart.

Dani took a bite of her food before speaking, her voice filled with newfound conviction. "Dad, I've been thinking a lot about what you said yesterday. I understand the risks, but I believe that embracing the teachings of the Overlords is the right path. It's our duty to serve them and maintain order in Dylath-Leen."

Larry looked at Dani, a mixture of conflicting emotions crossing his face. He admired her growth and resilience, her ability to adapt and find purpose within the constraints they lived in. Yet, he couldn't shake off his concerns about the true intentions of the Overlords and the potential loss of individual freedom.

"Dani, I'm proud of you for finding your own sense of purpose," Larry responded cautiously, his voice tinged with uneasiness. "But remember, it's important to remain vigilant and question everything. Blind loyalty can sometimes lead to unforeseen consequences."

Dani paused, her eyes searching her father's face. She understood the weight of his words and the caution behind them. "I know, Dad. I won't forget the importance of critical thinking. I'll keep questioning and seeking the truth within the boundaries we live in."

Larry nodded, appreciating Dani's willingness to maintain a balanced perspective. "That's all I ask, Dani. Stay true to yourself, never lose your sense of integrity, and always trust your instincts."

Their conversation continued, as they shared their thoughts on various aspects of life in Dylath-Leen. Larry couldn't help but feel a mixture of pride and concern for his daughter. He wanted her to find her own path, but he also feared the consequences of being too outspoken or challenging the established order.

As they finished their meal, Larry's cell phone went off. It was Sergeant Whately.

He answered the phone.

"What's up, Horace?"

"Hey, Boss," Horace said on the other end of the line. "We got another one."

"Alright. Where is it?"

The address Horace provided was only a few blocks away. Larry told Horace that he would be there soon, and hung up the phone.

"What's going on?" Dani asked.

"I've got to go to work for a while. Finish your homework and go to bed."

"Aww... Do I have to?"

"You know what time you need to be in bed."

"Fine," Dani said, sticking out her tongue. "I'll do my homework and then go to bed."

"Thanks, honey. I'll try to be back as soon as I can."

¤

Larry walked outside and climbed into the Shantak. After a few minutes, he pulled in through the gate of a recently built mansion in Oriab. As soon as he parked the car, Horace came walking out the front door. He was a tall, hairy man in his mid forties. Despite his stature and imposing looks, he was one of the best detectives in the city.

"It's about time," Horace said. "The coroner's here, so we can go inside."

"What's the cause of death?" Larry asked, locking the car.

"Well that's what I wanted you to see," Horace said, leading him towards the front door. "Come on."

The two of them walked into the large mansion. A row of expensive cars lined the driveway. The foyer was large and opulent. Marble tiles made a pattern on the floor, and a grand staircase made a path up to the second floor.

"So who's the victim?"

"Robert Crouchman," Horace replied. "Local big shot."

They walked into the living room, where a man in a lab coat was waiting. He looked at Larry expectantly.

"Horace, who's this?"

"Inspector Nodens," Horace said.

"I'm Dr. Pickman," the man in the lab coat said, thrusting his hand at Larry, who shook it.

"What can you tell me about the victim, doctor."

"The cause of death was a claw wounds to the chest and abdomen."

They followed the doctor into the victim's bedroom.

Robert Crouchman lay motionless on the luxurious, ornate bed in his bedroom. His pale, lifeless body was tinged with a hint of blue, indicating the onset of death. Crouchman was a middle-aged man with fair skin, his features frozen in a mix of surprise and terror. His eyes stared wide open, reflecting the horror of his final moments, while his mouth hung slightly ajar, forever silenced.

The cause of his demise was evident upon closer inspection. Deep, savage claw wounds marred his chest and abdomen, their jagged edges evidence of a brutal attack. The wounds had torn through his clothing, exposing his injured flesh. Blood stained his clothes and pooled beneath his lifeless form, stark red against the opulent backdrop of the bed.

The ghastly wounds inflicted upon Robert Crouchman spoke of a violent struggle, the ferocity of which was difficult to fathom. It was a chilling sight, a stark reminder of the fragility of life and the suddenness with which it could be extinguished.

As Larry approached the body, he couldn't help but feel a mix of curiosity and unease. While the death of a human was always a tragedy, the presence of claw wounds and the eerie circumstances surrounding the murder added an air of mystery and danger to the investigation.

"The other victim is in the study," Horace said with an element of anticipation.

¤

In the study, a chilling sight awaited the investigators. Lying lifeless on the floor was the body of an Overlord, a formidable alien creature known for its distinct features. The Overlord's blue fur, vibrant and tinged with a hint of luminescence, covered its four muscular arms, each one bearing a sense of power and strength. The lifeless eyes, once filled with intelligence and authority, now stared into nothingness.

"Is that an Overlord?!!" Larry said with awe.

"Yep," Frank Belknap said. "Definitely an Overlord."

Larry walked up to the body and took a closer look. Few people had seen an Overlord up close. And no one had ever seen a dead one.

The Overlord's body lay sprawled on the floor, its limbs twisted in unnatural positions. Its regal stature and imposing presence had been reduced to a lifeless shell, a victim of a heinous crime. The victim's eyes were frozen in terror, his mouth slightly open. Looking down at its chest, he saw a gaping wound. It went all the way through the sternum, exposing the massive blue heart. The wound was raw and gruesome, a testament to the brutal force behind the attack.

"What do you think caused the wounds?"

The doctor picked up a plastic bag containing curved sword. The blade was a dull silver with an ornate pattern running the length of it. The handle was black, with a purple gemstone in the hilt.

"This was found underneath the body," the doctor said.

"What is that, some sort of knife?" Larry asked.

"It's a Khopesh," Dr. Pickman said.

"The kind they used in Sarnath?"

"Exactly. It's a curved sword that was commonly used by the Sarnath raiders. People who got raided by them all the time called them Flints for the sound they made."

"Is it a real one or a knock-off?"

"It's the real thing. They haven't used these for a few hundred years, but from what I can tell, it's about 500 years old and made before the time of the Guild.

"Maybe Crouchman was a collector and the perp just used what was handy."

"Maybe, but I doubt it. Most of the folks who have these are collectors. I can't imagine Crouchman being one."

"Why not?"

"He's a legendary pacifist," Horace said. "He's written a few books on the subject. I can't imagine him owning something so aggressive unless he was into historical weaponry."

"This is unprecedented," Dr. Belknap murmured, his voice tinged with disbelief. "To witness the demise of an Overlord ruler, slain by an ancient Sarnath Khopesh sword... It's beyond anything we've ever encountered."

"Thanks, Doc."

Chapter 12

Larry and Horace walked back into the foyer.

"Horace, have the uniforms search for any other weaponry, historical or otherwise, on the premises. I don't expect they'll find any."

"Yes sir."

Larry walked into the drawing room, and found that several of the technicians had been hard at work.

"Have you found anything interesting?"

The lead technician, a short, balding man with spectacles looked up from his bench.

"I'm sorry, sir, but this is a crime scene. You can't be here."

"What have you found?"

The technician hesitated.

"I can't tell you," he said.

"I'm the lead investigator. Tell me what you've got!"

The technician sighed.

"We've found several fingerprints. We're running them through the database. If any of them come up positive, we'll have our culprit."

"What else? Come on, I know there's more."

The technician looked around, as if to make sure no one else was listening, then leaned in.

"There are some hairs stuck in the blood," he said."

"What kind of hairs?"

"Human," he says, "but not modern ones."

"What do you mean?"

The technician stood and pulled a small plastic bag out of his lab coat pocket, slipping it into Larry's hand.

"I mean they're not human hairs from this era. I'm pretty sure these are Neanderthal hairs."

Larry looked at the hairs in the bag.

"What makes you think that?"

"The curvature of the hair," he said.

"I see. Do any modern era beings have similar hair?"

"Maybe some mammals that are closely related to humans, like apes or something. But these would be too short. The hairs in the blood have been shaved."

"Thanks for the information,"

Larry headed down the hall to the study, where he assumed Crouchman kept any files related to his work.

The room was dark, as the technicians had been unable to find the switch for the lighting.

Larry felt around and flicked the lights on. He walked over to a large oak desk and pushed aside various papers hoping to find anything related to Claire Noble or her clones.

On the desk, he found a drawing of one of the clones, a pen-and-ink drawing of Crouchman, a collection of short stories Crouchman wrote in his youth, and a small pile of documents.

Larry read through the stack. The first was an old, handwritten letter from Crouchman's mother to a friend. It pertained to domestic matters and had no bearing on the case.

The next was a collection of short stories, essays, and other works of fiction and nonfiction that Crouchman had written while in college. Some of the handwriting was hard to read, but he understood the majority of it.

Larry picked up the final item, a photograph. He studied it. It depicted Crouchman, a woman whose face he recognized from pictures in the hallway as Crouchman's mother, and a young, dark-haired woman with her arm around Crouchman. The hair was not blond, but Larry was positive it was one of the clones.

He sat down at the desk and made some notes, trying to organize his thoughts.

Did one of the clones kill Crouchman? The one in the photograph? One of the others?

Or was Crouchman somehow connected to the clones and the clone killer got him too. Why would he do that?

No matter what, Larry was going to have to find the clone. It was either Heather Jensen, Susan Jones, or Lisa Taylor.

He left the study.

"Any signs of weaponry, Horace?"

"None," he said. "We didn't find anything."

"Thanks."

"Any conclusions?"

Larry shook his head. "But he knew one of the clones."

"What makes you think that?"

"I found this photograph of one of them in his study."

"Really?" Horace asks. "We didn't find it."

"It was buried on the desk under a bunch of old stories that he wrote. And she dyed her hair black."

"Lisa?" Horace said.

"You mean Lisa Taylor?"

"Yes. Do you think it's Lisa?"

"Maybe. What do we know about Lisa?"

"Nothing."

"Well, we know she was a police officer. I'll have Gwen go through the DLPD personnel system."

"You think she's still alive?"

"Maybe, maybe not. We need to know what we're facing."

"I think we've found all we're going to here. I'm going to brief the CoCID, and then the Overlord Authority will probably take over the case."

¤

The implications of an Overlord being murdered sent shockwaves through him. It meant that the delicate balance of power and coexistence between humans and the extraterrestrial beings had been shattered. The stakes were high, and the atmosphere grew tense as Larry absorbed the gravity of the situation. Larry knew that the secretive Overlord Authority would likely take over the case as they did with anything directly dealing with the Overlords.

Larry quickly reached for his phone and dialed Superintendent Gaunt's number. As the phone rang, he could feel the weight of the situation pressing upon him, the urgency of the investigation driving his actions. After a few moments, Gaunt answered the call, her voice steady and composed.

"Superintendent Gaunt," she said, her tone businesslike and efficient.

"CoCID, it's Inspector Nodens," Larry said, his voice reflecting a mix of urgency and concern. "We've had two significant deaths that require immediate attention," Larry began, his voice carrying a sense of urgency. "First, Robert Crouchman, a prominent figure in the city. He was found dead in his bedroom, viciously attacked with claw wounds to his chest and abdomen. It's a brutal and puzzling case."

Gaunt's response was measured, devoid of any discernible emotion. "I see. And what's the other death?"

Larry continued, "The second case is even more unsettling. In the study, we found the body of an Overlord, one of the city's alien rulers. This Overlord was killed by an ancient Sarnath Khopesh sword, with a deep wound to the chest that exposed the heart. It's an unprecedented crime, Superintendent. The implications are significant."

There was a brief pause on the other end of the line before Gaunt responded. "I understand the gravity of the situation, Inspector. You are to secure the scene immediately, making sure no evidence is disturbed or compromised. Gather up any collected evidence and make preparations to hand it over to the Overlord Authority when they arrive. They will be taking the lead on this matter."

Larry nodded, even though Gaunt couldn't see him. "Understood, CoCID. I will ensure the scene is properly secured, and all evidence will be handed over to the Overlord Authority as per your instructions."

Gaunt's voice remained stoic and commanding. "Good. This is a delicate situation, Inspector. Maintain clear lines of communication with the Overlord Authority and cooperate fully with their investigation. Keep me updated on any significant developments."

"I will, CoCID," Larry affirmed, a sense of determination filling his voice.

"Remember, Inspector, we need to tread carefully. The murder of an Overlord has far-reaching implications. We cannot afford any missteps or mistakes."

"I understand, Superintendent. I will proceed with utmost caution and diligence."

With that, the conversation ended, leaving Larry with a renewed sense of purpose. He knew that the investigation had taken an unprecedented turn, and the delicate balance between humans and Overlords hung in the balance.

¤

The sound of approaching footsteps echoed through the hallway, drawing his attention. Moments later, a group of agents from the Overlord Authority entered the room, their presence commanding attention and authority.

One of the agents, a stern-faced man, stepped forward, addressing Larry. "Inspector Nodens, as representatives of the Overlord Authority, we are assuming control of this investigation. The murder of the Overlord is beyond your jurisdiction."

Larry's brow furrowed with a mix of confusion and concern. While the involvement of the Overlord Authority was not entirely unexpected given the nature of the case, the abrupt removal of CID from the investigation raised questions about their autonomy and the sharing of information.

"Sir, we have made significant progress in the investigation," Larry began, attempting to assert CID's capabilities and expertise. "We understand the complexities involved and have been working closely with Dr. Belknap, the medical examiner, to gather evidence and insights."

The agent raised a hand, cutting Larry off mid-sentence. "Inspector Nodens, your efforts are appreciated, but this matter now falls under the jurisdiction of the Overlord Authority. We have our own protocols and resources in place to handle such cases. Your cooperation is expected."

Suppressing his frustration, Larry acknowledged the authority of the covert Overlord Authority. "Understood, sir. We will cooperate and provide any assistance necessary to ensure a thorough investigation."

The agents from the covert Overlord Authority began to take charge, directing the CID investigators to step back and hand over their findings and evidence. As the dynamics of the investigation shifted, Larry couldn't help but feel a mix of disappointment and curiosity about the depth of the covert Overlord Authority's involvement and the secrets they held.

As the covert Overlord Authority took control of the investigation, Larry and his team reluctantly stepped aside, hoping that their earlier progress would be acknowledged and factored into the ongoing investigation. The road ahead remained uncertain, but Larry remained resolute in his commitment to the truth, even if it meant navigating through unfamiliar territories alongside the covert Overlord Authority.

Chapter 13

Larry woke up to the energetic sound of Dani bouncing on her bed, signaling the start of a new day.

"Morning, Dad!" she greeted him cheerfully.

Larry couldn't help but smile at her enthusiasm. "Good morning! Why are you so cheerful today?"

Dani shrugged, a gleam of happiness in her eyes. "No reason, I guess. I just am."

As Larry headed into the kitchen to prepare some coffee, Dani poked her head in, offering a suggestion. "You should go to work. I'll do my homework and take the bus to school."

Larry chuckled at her attempt to take charge. "Are you trying to get rid of me? Remember, I'm a detective."

Dani laughed and reassured him. "I'll be fine, Dad. I'm a big girl now."

With the coffee brewing, Larry finished his morning routine. "Okay, I'll leave you to it. I'm going to work."

He grabbed his keys and headed towards the door, bidding Dani farewell. "See you later, honey."

"See you later, Dad," Dani replied, her voice filled with warmth.

Stepping into his car, Larry checked his phone and noticed three missed calls, all from Gwen. Concern crept into his mind as he dialed her number, only to be met with silence.

"Something's not right," Larry muttered to himself, feeling a growing unease. He dialed Alan's number next, knowing he would likely be at the precinct.

"Hello?" Alan's voice came through the phone.

"Alan, it's Nodens. Are you at the precinct?" Larry inquired urgently.

"Yeah, I'm here. What's up?" Alan responded.

"I've been trying to reach Gwen, but she's not answering. Have you seen her?"

Alan's tone turned grave. "You too, huh? She's not responding to me either. I'm considering heading over to her place to make sure she's alright."

"I'm already in my car. I'll swing by on my way to the precinct," Larry offered, sensing the urgency.

"Thanks," Alan sighed. "I'll see you in a few minutes then." Ending the call, Larry redirected his route towards Gwen's house.

¤

Larry approached Gwen's house, growing increasingly concerned when he received no response to his calls.

Upon arrival, he knocked on the door, but there was no response. The worry deepened within him, heightening his determination to uncover the truth.

"Gwen? It's Larry. Are you there?" he called out, straining his ears for any sign of activity but receiving only silence in return.

Feeling a sense of urgency, Larry's worry intensified. He noticed the window beside the door and decided to take matters into his own hands.

"Gwen!" he shouted, knocking on the window. "If you're in there, I'm breaking in."

Stepping back, Larry braced himself and forcefully rammed his shoulder into the window. It shattered, and he tumbled inside, landing on the carpeted floor.

Shaking off the impact, Larry quickly surveyed the living room, finding everything seemingly in order. He proceeded down the hallway, checking the closed bedroom doors until he reached Gwen's room, which was wide open.

Entering cautiously, he called out her name. His eyes widened as he spotted Gwen lying unconscious on the floor next to her bed, dressed in pajamas. Her phone lay nearby on the floor.

Rushing to her side, Larry checked her pulse and found that she was still alive. Acting swiftly, he dialed Alan's number, and to his relief, Alan answered after just one ring.

"Hello?" Alan's voice sounded concerned.

"Gwen's at her place, unconscious. I'm calling for an ambulance," Larry informed him urgently.

"I'll meet you there. I'm on my way," Alan replied, his determination evident.

Ending the call, Larry dialed 911, seeking immediate medical assistance.

"911, what is your emergency?" the operator asked calmly.

"This is Inspector Nodens. One of my detectives is unconscious in her home. Send an ambulance!" Larry pleaded urgently.

The operator's tone remained composed. "I'm sorry, sir. Can you please calm down and tell me what your emergency is?"

Larry took a deep breath, trying to steady his voice. "My name is Larry Nodens. I'm a CID Inspector. My subordinate, Gwen Pabodie, is unconscious. I need an ambulance."

The operator asked for the address, and Larry provided it promptly. Assured that help was on the way, he sat by Gwen's side, holding her hand, while waiting for the ambulance to arrive.

Moments later, the front door burst open, and Alan rushed in, visibly worried.

"Nodens! Are you okay?" Alan called out, seeking reassurance.

Larry nodded, grateful for his colleague's swift response. "Yeah. How did you get here so quickly?"

Alan checked Gwen's condition, then glanced at his phone. "I was already on my way."

The wailing sirens drew closer, announcing the arrival of the ambulance.

"That must be them," Alan remarked.

"I instructed them to come in. I had to break into the house," Larry explained, his concern clear on his face.

Alan expressed his gratitude. "Thank you, Larry. Thank you for looking out for her."

Determined to ensure Gwen's safety, Larry investigated further. "I'll search for any signs of an intruder."

Larry combed through the house, his senses heightened. After a thorough inspection, he discovered the backdoor was open, although there were no visible signs of forced entry.

"Alan," Larry called out, standing in the kitchen. "Alan, come look at this."

Curiosity piqued, Alan joined Larry in the kitchen, where Larry pointed to the open back door.

"The lock is intact. There are no signs of forced entry," Larry observed, puzzled.

Alan nodded, equally perplexed. "That doesn't make any sense."

Agreeing with Alan's sentiment, Larry stepped outside and surveyed the surroundings, searching for any clues. Fences bordered the small yard on either side, with a row of bushes on the left and the road leading to Gwen's parking spot on the right.

"I don't see any footprints or signs of an intruder," Larry reported.

Alan's thoughts aligned with Larry's. "Maybe we can rule out an intruder. Perhaps it's a medical emergency like a heart attack or a seizure."

Larry's mind, however, remained skeptical. "Maybe, but Gwen doesn't believe in coincidences."

Alan nodded in agreement. "Neither do I. Something strange is going on."

The gravity of the situation weighed heavily on both of them as they stood in contemplative silence.

Interrupting their thoughts, a paramedic appeared at the door, announcing their arrival.

"We're taking her to Dylath Hospital," the paramedic informed them.

Larry walked outside, climbing into the ambulance with Gwen, while Alan followed in his car. The journey to the hospital was filled with an uneasy silence.

"This doesn't feel right," Larry expressed his unease, his voice laden with concern and determination to uncover the truth.

¤

After a few minutes of tense silence, the ambulance arrived at Dylath Hospital. The paramedic swiftly unloaded Gwen from the back and began wheeling her into the hospital, with Alan arriving shortly after.

They followed a nurse through the hospital corridors and entered a room with several beds. The paramedic transferred Gwen onto one of the beds, ready to hand over her care to the medical staff.

"I'll leave her in your care," the paramedic informed the nurse before they both exited the room, leaving Larry and Alan alone with Gwen. Alan sat by her side, holding her hand, while Larry remained restless.

"Nodens," Alan said, his voice firm. "Come sit down."

Larry hesitated, his mind consumed by the need to investigate. "I can't just sit here. We need to find out what happened. We need to investigate!"

Alan's voice carried a tone of authority. "Larry, sit down."

Taking a deep breath, Larry complied and settled into the nearest chair. The two of them sat in an uneasy silence, waiting for news in the hospital room.

A doctor entered the room, a short, balding man.

"I'm Dr. Barzai," he introduced himself. "Are you Gwen's partner?" he asked, directing his question to both Alan and Larry.

"Yes," Alan confirmed, and Larry nodded in agreement.

The doctor seated himself at a desk, typing on a tablet. "Tell me what happened. Provide me with all the details."

Larry and Alan exchanged a brief glance, unsure of where to start. Sensing their uncertainty, the doctor offered an assumption.

"Taking a guess," the doctor began, "I'd think you would start with when you found her."

Alan took the lead in responding. "Miss Pabodie didn't show up for work, so I went to her house and discovered her unconscious. That's when I called for an ambulance."

The doctor nodded, his attention focused on the tablet. "And what is your relationship to the patient?"

"I'm her Inspector, and we're all police detectives," Larry answered.

Dr. Barzai continued his inquiry. "How long has she been unconscious?"

"Since I found her," Larry replied.

The doctor's gaze shifted between Larry and Alan, then back to the tablet. "According to the information here, she was found approximately two hours ago. Why weren't you aware of her unconsciousness for such a long time?"

Larry felt the weight of the doctor's scrutiny but maintained his composure. "I came to check on her when she didn't show up for work. I discovered her unconscious in her bedroom and immediately called for an ambulance."

Dr. Barzai studied Larry's face intently before shifting his focus to Alan. His next question took them by surprise.

"Were there any open wounds when you found her? Any signs of cuts or blood?"

Confused, Alan sought clarification. "Excuse me?"

"Did you notice any injuries on her body? Was there any bleeding?" the doctor elaborated.

"No," Alan responded, perplexed. "We didn't see any signs of injury."

The doctor made a note on his tablet. The room fell into silence for a moment before he continued.

"I need to ask you both a few questions about her general health," Dr. Barzai stated. "Are either of you aware if she had any medication allergies?"

Larry pondered for a moment. "I don't think so."

Nodding, the doctor typed on his tablet. "Did she have any known illnesses or medical conditions?"

"Not to my knowledge," Larry offered. "She joined my team only a couple of months ago."

The doctor made another notation on his tablet. A brief silence followed before Larry spoke up.

"Is there a diagnosis? What happened to her?"

Suddenly, Gwen's eyes fluttered open, interrupting the conversation.

"What...?" she muttered, her voice weak and confused. She shook her head slightly. "What happened?"

"We found you on the floor of your bedroom," Alan gently explained. "Do you remember anything?"

Gwen's response came groggily. "Yeah, I remember getting out of bed." She slowly sat up.

"I'm going to be fine, right?" she asked, seeking reassurance.

"Of course," Alan reassured her. "You just need some rest, and then you'll be back to your usual self."

Gwen nodded, settling back down and closing her eyes. "I'm tired," she murmured.

"Yeah," Larry agreed softly. "We'll let you get some sleep."

They stood up and quietly exited the room. As they left, Dr. Barzai addressed them.

"We'll run some tests and see if we can find anything. I'll contact you when we have more information."

"Thank you, doctor," Larry acknowledged with gratitude.

"Alan, let's go secure Gwen's house," Larry directed.

"On it, boss," Alan replied, ready to take action.

Larry left the hospital, riding with Alan back to Gwen's house, and then made his way to the Police Presidium, determined to continue the investigation.

¤

Larry settled into his office, sinking into his desk chair with a heavy sigh. The stack of papers in his inbox demanded his attention, but he found himself lost in thought. Just as he was about to tackle the paperwork, Horace entered the room.

"Hey, boss," Horace greeted him. "I just talked to Alan. He filled me in on what happened with Gwen."

Larry leaned back in his chair, weariness etched on his face. "Could be nothing. No signs of forced entry, though the back door was open. And no visible injuries."

Horace nodded in agreement. "Yeah, we discussed that over the phone."

Larry's eyes narrowed, his mind racing to find an explanation. "What do you think caused it?"

Horace's response caught Larry off guard. "I think she had a heart attack."

Larry stared at him, a mixture of disbelief and concern on his face. "You don't seriously believe that, do you? She's only twenty-eight. Young people don't typically have heart attacks without external causes. Are you suggesting the stress of this precinct triggered it?"

Horace shrugged, uncertainty lining his features. "Maybe. Do you have a better explanation?"

Frustrated, Larry changed the subject. "What progress have we made on the case?"

Horace sighed and handed Larry a stack of papers. "We don't have much to go on. These are the reports from witnesses and bystanders we interviewed."

Larry quickly scanned through the reports, searching for any leads. One report stood out from a hiker named David Ackerson, who claimed to have witnessed a gray sedan speeding away from the crime scene when Claire Noble was murdered.

"Anything else?" Larry asked, his gaze fixed on Horace.

Horace shook his head. "That's pretty much it. No other witnesses or significant leads."

Larry's attention turned to potential suspects. "What about suspects? Anyone of interest?"

Horace hesitated before responding. "Well, there's one, but the connection is weak. Ewan Conner. He's had prior arrests for similar crimes."

"A Peeping Tom?" Larry questioned.

Horace's voice turned serious. "No, a rapist."

Larry's expression hardened as he decided. "Let's bring him in. We need to see what he knows."

Chapter 14

Horace led Larry to the interrogation room where Ewan Conner, a young man, sat at the table.

"Ewan Conner?" Larry addressed him.

Ewan glared at Larry. "That's me."

Larry introduced himself and Horace. "I'm Inspector Nodens, and this is Sergeant Whately."

Ewan responded sarcastically, "How do you do?"

Larry began the questioning. "Can you tell us where you were on the night of January sixth?"

Ewan's demeanor shifted, his gaze shifting away. "I was at home. I live alone, so I guess my neighbors can confirm that."

Larry pressed further. "Do you have any witnesses who can vouch for your whereabouts between nine PM and five AM?"

Ewan grew defensive. "No. I was alone in my home, and I believe my right to privacy allows me not to provide an alibi for that time period."

Larry's patience waned. "Those rights went out with the Overlords. You need to prove your innocence."

Ewan scoffed. "Yeah, yeah. I forgot we live in a dictatorship."

"So, you're saying you weren't out committing a crime?" Larry challenged.

Ewan maintained his stance. "I wasn't. Like I said, I was at home. In bed. Alone."

Larry confronted Ewan with the witness statement. "We have a witness who saw a car similar to yours leaving one of the crime scenes at high speed."

Ewan burst into laughter. "What? Sorry, but I drove my car to a house party and went straight back home that night. I didn't leave my house until the next afternoon. You can check my odometer if you don't believe me."

Larry's questioning continued. "And you have no idea what happened to Claire?"

Ewan's tone softened. "No, I barely knew her. She was a nice girl, though."

Larry concluded the interrogation. "Okay, we'll be in touch if we have more questions."

Larry and Horace left Ewan alone in the interrogation room.

¤

"What now?" Horace asked.

Larry pondered for a moment. "He just admitted the car was his, but I don't think he's our serial killer."

Horace chimed in. "Yeah, but if he's nervous, maybe he's hiding something."

Larry considered the options. "Do you want to stay and question him further?"

Horace nodded determinedly. "If you don't mind, I'd like to stay here a little longer. There might be something more we can uncover."

"Fine. I'm going to report to CoCID."

"Sounds good. I'll be here for a while," Horace confirmed.

Larry left the interrogation room, heading towards the CoCID office, determined to gather more information and find the real perpetrator.

¤

¤

Larry walked back to the squad room, a sense of urgency driving him. He approached the door of Superintendent Gaunt's office and knocked.

"Come in," came the reply from inside. Larry opened the door and entered, finding Superintendent Gaunt seated behind her desk.

"Inspector Nodens. Report," she said, her tone firm.

Larry took a deep breath and began, "There have been significant developments in the case, CoCID. We have identified the six clones, but we've also discovered another individual connected to them. She claims to be Claire Noble's twin and did not know of the other clones."

Superintendent Gaunt leaned forward, her eyes focused. "How many clones are we talking about here?"

"We have identified a total of six clones based on the lab records," Larry responded.

Superintendent Gaunt's expression turned grave. "So, where are the other five?"

"Three of them are deceased. The first victim was Susan Jones, a recording artist. Claire Noble, whom we believe to be the original, was the second victim. Allison Craven was the third. Our fourth victim is Jennifer Allen, another clone. The remaining clones are Heather Jensen, a doctor, Lisa Taylor, an alleged police officer, and Karen Stone, a cook."

Superintendent Gaunt sighed. "That's quite a list."

Larry nodded, his gaze unwavering. "Indeed. We've also gathered additional information regarding the crime scenes."

"Tell me more," Superintendent Gaunt urged.

"We found pills on Claire Noble's person. Surprisingly, we discovered a prescription for the same drug on Jennifer Allen. The prescription was issued by a Dr. Llanfer from a place called The Facility. We attempted to interview Dr. Llanfer, but he was uncooperative, so we've detained him and his staff. Currently, we are searching the the building. It's worth noting that Dr. Llanfer's staff includes a separate set of clones."

Superintendent Gaunt's brows furrowed. "How many sets of clones have you found?"

"Just one set among the staff. However, Dr. Llanfer mentioned that other clones were created and sold as slaves, prostitutes, or for use in snuff films."

"He actually admitted that?" Superintendent Gaunt questioned.

"Yes, though he refused to provide any further details until we apprehended him. He's been continuously repeating, 'You don't want to know the truth.' He's clearly mentally unstable."

Superintendent Gaunt leaned back in her chair, processing the information. "You mentioned another person. Who is she?"

"Megan Green. She's not one of the clones, but she bears a striking resemblance to them. She was stabbed in the neck two months ago."

Superintendent Gaunt's eyes lit up with intrigue. "Interesting. Anything else?"

"That brings me to our most recent victim, Robert Crouchman. He was not a clone but possibly a buyer. He was fatally stabbed in the heart with a Sarnath Khopesh."

Superintendent Gaunt's eyebrows shot up. "A what?"

"A Sarnath Khopesh. It's a curved sword used by the Sarnath raiders, a group that existed five hundred years ago before their city was destroyed. The weapon is incredibly rare and valuable."

Superintendent Gaunt frowned. "What would a relic of the raiders be doing in this case?"

"I don't have the answer yet, but it's a peculiar choice of weapon, and it's strange that the killer would leave behind such a distinctive and valuable clue."

Superintendent Gaunt nodded thoughtfully. "I see. Anything else to report?"

"That's all for now," Larry confirmed.

Superintendent Gaunt acknowledged his efforts. "Interesting developments, Inspector. Keep up the good work, and inform me immediately if you uncover any further details."

"Oh, one more thing. Detective Pabodie was found unconscious in her house. She has been taken to Dylath Hospital, and Detective Gillman is with her."

Superintendent Gaunt's expression turned concerned. "I see. Thank you for informing me. Keep me updated on her condition."

Larry left Superintendent Gaunt's office, his mind buzzing with thoughts. He made his way to his car, determined to head to Dylath Hospital and gather more information about Detective Pabodie's condition. The pieces of the puzzle were slowly coming together, and he was resolved to solve the mystery that lay before them.

¤

Larry parked his car and made his way into the hospital lobby. Spotting a nurse, he approached her and inquired about Gwen Pabodie's whereabouts. The nurse provided him with a room number, and Larry proceeded down the hallway toward that room. As he entered, he found Alan seated by Gwen's bedside, his eyes fixed on her sleeping form. Alan glanced up as Larry walked in.

"Oh, hi," Alan greeted, his voice filled with a mix of exhaustion and concern.

"Any news?" Larry asked, his voice filled with anticipation.

"You're not going to believe this," Alan began, his tone incredulous. "She's pregnant. She collapsed because she hasn't been eating for two."

Larry's eyes widened in surprise. "What?"

Alan nodded, a mixture of bewilderment and worry on his face. "Yeah. She's been experiencing morning sickness and vomiting. It turns out she's about two months pregnant, which means it happened just before she joined our team."

Larry's mind raced as he processed the information. "Does she know who the father is?"

Alan sighed, his expression filled with concern. "She says it's me."

Larry was taken aback by the revelation. "Oh, I didn't know you two were previously involved."

Alan nodded, his worry deepening. "Yeah, we have a history."

"That's... great," Larry responded, struggling to find the right words in the face of this unexpected revelation.

"Listen, I want to ask you for a favor," Alan spoke up, his voice tinged with vulnerability.

"Sure, anything," Larry offered.

Alan looked at him earnestly. "Could you stay here with me? Just until she wakes up? I don't want to be alone right now."

Larry's face softened with empathy. "Of course, Alan. I'll stay by your side. You're not alone."

"Thanks," Alan murmured, mustering a faint smile of gratitude.

Taking a seat in a nearby chair, Larry settled in next to Alan. He reached out and gently held Gwen's hand, a silent gesture of support. Together, they waited for Gwen to awaken, their thoughts and emotions intertwined in this unexpected turn of events.

Chapter 15

After approximately an hour, Gwen's eyelids fluttered, and she regained consciousness.

"Where am I?" she asked, her voice filled with confusion.

"You're in the hospital," Alan replied, concern evident in his tone.

"What happened?" Gwen inquired, her memory still hazy.

"You passed out," Alan explained, trying to reassure her.

Gwen took a moment to absorb the information, her eyes widening with a sudden realization.

"The baby! Is the baby okay?" she exclaimed, worry marring her face.

"Yes, Gwen. The baby is fine," Alan reassured her, hoping to ease her fears.

Gwen visibly relaxed, finding solace in the news about her unborn child.

"What's going on? What happened?" she asked, seeking answers.

Alan glanced at Larry, silently asking for help in explaining the situation. Larry understood the unspoken request and stepped in.

"You've been under a lot of stress lately, Gwen," Larry began gently. "We've all been dealing with high levels of pressure. Perhaps that took a toll on your health. You should have reached out for help. I was so worried when I found you."

Gwen looked perplexed, struggling to comprehend the situation.

"Alan, I don't understand," she voiced her confusion.

"For now, what's important is that you focus on getting better," Alan interjected, his voice filled with concern. "The doctors want to keep you here until you're stable and properly nourished."

"I... I don't know how this happened," Gwen whispered, her voice laced with sadness and confusion.

"You don't have to worry about that right now," Larry responded, his voice gentle yet firm. "Your priority is to take care of yourself and the baby. Get some rest, Gwen. We'll check on you tomorrow."

Gwen nodded weakly, appreciating their concern and assurance.

"We'll be back tomorrow," Larry reiterated.

"Thank you, Sir," Gwen replied with a faint smile.

Exiting the hospital room, Larry and Alan walked together towards their cars, both lost in their thoughts. The silence persisted until they reached Alan's vehicle.

"Alan," Larry spoke up, breaking the silence. "I can't let her go back to work, not in this condition."

Alan nodded, acknowledging the gravity of the situation. "I know."

"But that means you'll have to handle her data analysis as well. I need you to stay on top of things," Larry continued, emphasizing the importance of their work.

"I understand. It's just..." Alan trailed off, staring off into the distance as he contemplated the challenges ahead.

"What is it?" Larry pressed, concerned for his partner's well-being.

"This won't be easy for me," Alan admitted after a moment, his voice tinged with vulnerability. "Impending fatherhood, Gwen in the hospital, extra workload."

"I'll see if I can get someone from CoCID to assist us. But until then, you're it," Larry replied firmly, determined to find a solution.

"Thanks," Alan said, his tone carrying a mix of gratitude and resignation. "I'll try to work something out. I need to get back to the office, anyway."

Larry offered a supportive pat on Alan's shoulder before making his way to his own car, leaving Alan to process the weight of the responsibility that lay ahead.

¤

Larry made his way to the Police Presidium and headed straight for the CoCID's office. He knocked on the door, waiting for permission to enter.

"Come in!" Superintendent Gaunt's voice rang out from inside.

Larry stepped into the office, maintaining a professional demeanor.

"Inspector Nodens. Report!" Gaunt commanded.

"Detective Pabodie is pregnant and will be hospitalized for an extended period. I require a replacement data analyst," Larry reported, getting straight to the point.

Gaunt took a moment to consider the request, poring over the papers on her desk. Her face reflected deep thought as she contemplated the suitable candidate.

"What about Henry Armitage?" she suggested after a brief pause.

Larry furrowed his brows, unfamiliar with the name. He wondered if Armitage possessed the necessary skills for the job.

"Who is he?" Larry inquired, seeking more information.

"He's one of our most skilled analysts. Granted, he may be on the older side, but his expertise could prove invaluable," Gaunt explained.

Larry considered the suggestion, weighing the pros and cons of having an experienced yet potentially older analyst.

"Is there anyone with a more contemporary skill set?" Larry questioned, hoping for a candidate who would be up to date with the latest analytical techniques.

Gaunt scanned through her papers once again, searching for an alternative candidate.

"Well, there is one other possibility," Gaunt revealed, looking down at her notes. "Farley Lake."

The name didn't ring a bell for Larry, but he trusted Gaunt's judgment.

"And what do you know about Farley Lake?" Larry asked, curious about this potential candidate.

Gaunt paused, collecting her thoughts before responding.

"Lake is a competent analyst, well-versed in the required skills. They may not have as much experience as Armitage, but their knowledge and abilities are commendable," Gaunt elaborated.

Larry nodded, realizing that Lake might be a suitable choice despite their lesser experience.

"They sound like a promising option," Larry conceded, acknowledging Gaunt's recommendation.

"Very well," Gaunt said, making a note on her paperwork. "I'll have Lake report to you immediately."

"Thank you, sir," Larry expressed his gratitude, appreciating Gaunt's swift action.

"Is there anything else?" Gaunt inquired, looking up from her papers.

"No, that's all for now," Larry replied. "I'll handle the rest. Thank you again, sir."

With their conversation concluded, Larry turned to leave the office, ready to welcome the new data analyst and tackle the challenges that lay ahead.

¤

Larry returned to his office, ready to dive into his work. As he began sorting through his inbox, a knock on the door interrupting his concentration. He called out for the person to enter, and in walked a young woman, approximately 30 years old, wearing a long black leather coat and sporting short brown hair.

"Detective Lake reporting for duty, sir," she announced confidently.

Larry couldn't help but steal a quick glance at her appearance, feeling a slight blush creeping up his cheeks. Trying to regain his composure, he gestured for her to take a seat.

"Hello, sir," she greeted him as she settled into the chair.

"Do you know why you're here, Detective?" Larry asked, trying to sound composed.

"I assume you need a data analyst," she replied.

"Yes, that's correct. Do you have any knowledge about the job or the situation at hand?" Larry inquired.

"I'm afraid I don't, sir," she admitted.

Larry paused, studying her intently. He wanted to ensure she understood the gravity of the situation before moving forward.

"I'll be honest with you, Detective. The situation is highly dangerous. There's a significant risk involved, and you may be putting your life on the line," Larry cautioned.

"Sounds like my kind of job, sir," she responded calmly, displaying a level of fearlessness.

"Where were you previously stationed?" Larry inquired, curious about her background.

"I served as a military analyst before joining the department, sir," she revealed.

"Ah, so you possess knowledge of strategy and tactics," Larry observed.

"That's correct, sir," she confirmed.

"Good," Larry acknowledged, satisfied with her background.

"We're currently pursuing a serial killer who has claimed the lives of five individuals. The killer's intent is to make the murders resemble the work of the Ravagers," Larry explained, summarizing the case.

"Hmm, so the killer is attempting to frame the Ravagers," Detective Lake deduced.

"Yes, precisely. Moreover, we believe the killer is specifically targeting a group of clones. These clones were part of an experiment authorized by the Overlords," Larry continued, revealing a crucial piece of information.

He paused briefly, realizing that he had shared more than he initially intended, but he decided it was necessary for Detective Lake to be fully informed.

"Three of the victims share identical characteristics: blond hair, blue eyes, and athletic builds. Of the other two victims, one wasn't a clone but bore a resemblance to them. Additionally, we suspect that the remaining victim was involved in the purchase of these clones. Our investigation has uncovered that clones were being 'grown' for purposes such as slavery, prostitution, and even exploitation in movies," Larry disclosed, providing her with essential details.

"I see. And what exactly do you want me to do?" Detective Lake inquired, her tone composed and attentive.

Larry explained the tasks he required her to undertake, carefully detailing the responsibilities she would assume. As he concluded, Detective Lake sat in thoughtful silence, absorbing the information.

"Your first assignment will involve searching the DLPD personnel database for an officer named Lisa Taylor. She is one of the clones. Compare the pictures in the case file with the database to determine her current whereabouts and recent activities. Any questions?" Larry clarified.

"No, sir," Detective Lake responded confidently.

"Very well," Larry acknowledged. "You can begin in the morning if you prefer, considering the late hour."

"I can start right now, sir. I don't mind," Detective Lake offered.

"As you wish, Detective," Larry agreed, appreciating her eagerness.

Larry handed her the case file containing eight photographs of the victims. He watched as she examined the pictures, her gaze focused and determined.

"Do you recognize any of them, Lake?" Larry asked, curious to hear her observations.

"Yes, sir. This one," she pointed to one of the unidentified photographs. "That's Lisa."

"Are you certain? Take another look at all of them," Larry prompted, wanting to ensure accuracy.

Detective Lake reviewed each picture once more, then turned her gaze back to Larry.

"Yes, I'm sure. That's her," she confirmed with confidence.

Larry pressed for more information, hoping to gain insight into her reasoning.

"How do you know?" he probed.

"I've worked on a few cases with her. I know her," Detective Lake replied, looking at Larry as if her familiarity with Lisa should be enough to convince him.

Larry paused, considering the significance of her claim.

"Do you have any knowledge of her current assignment or where she lives?" Larry asked, hoping for more information.

"I'm not certain about her current assignment, sir. However, I believe she lives somewhere in Ulthar," Detective Lake shared, providing the details she knew.

Larry sighed, feeling the weight of the task ahead of them, and stared at the file on his desk.

"Please locate her and ensure she reports here in the morning. That will be all, Detective," Larry instructed, emphasizing the importance of finding Lisa.

"Thank you, sir," Detective Lake acknowledged, rising from her seat.

She left the office, and Larry took a deep breath, attempting to refocus his thoughts. He leaned back in his chair, contemplating his next steps. Calling Superintendent Gaunt crossed his mind, but he decided it could wait until morning.

For the rest of the day, Larry busied himself with organizing his desk, sorting through case files, and preparing a comprehensive to-do list for the following morning.

¤

Realizing it was time to call it a day, Larry packed up to head home. He locked his office door and made his way toward the main exit. However, as he approached the glass door to the squad room, he noticed a figure standing beside it. It was Detective Lake.

Larry approached the door, and Detective Lake looked at him with an expectant gaze. He opened the door and gestured for her to exit.

"After you," Larry said, holding the door open for her.

Lake stepped outside and turned to face him.

"I was waiting for you, sir," she stated matter-of-factly.

Larry raised an eyebrow, slightly intrigued by her presence.

"Is that so?" he responded.

"Yes, sir," Lake replied stoically.

Curiosity piqued, Larry couldn't help but ask, "Is there something you need from me?"

"Yes, sir. I live at my aunt's house in Old Dylath. It's located near the old Jasmine Fields golf course," Lake revealed.

Larry appeared puzzled, wondering why she was sharing this information.

"Why are you telling me this? Am I supposed to pick you up or something?" he inquired.

A flicker of darkness crossed Lake's face briefly before returning to her composed demeanor.

"I was instructed to offer any assistance you may need, sir. If you require transportation or anything else, I can provide it for you. I don't sleep much, so feel free to call me anytime you need assistance. Please, sir, consider me at your service," Lake offered earnestly.

Larry couldn't believe what he was hearing, his surprise evident.

"Am I hearing what I think I'm hearing?" Larry asked, seeking clarification.

"You'll have to decide that, sir," Lake replied, turning to leave.

Larry stood in the parking lot, watching her depart, contemplating the situation.

"Where are you off to now?" Lake inquired without looking back.

"Home, of course," Larry replied.

Lake nodded in understanding.

"I'll walk you there then."

Larry, taken aback by her assertion, came up with an idea.

"Join me for dinner," he proposed.

"I'd be delighted, sir," Lake accepted without missing a beat.

Larry shook his head, realizing that sleep might elude him that night. Thankfully, he had completed his paperwork earlier in the day.

"We'll take your car, sir," Lake suggested as they approached Larry's vehicle, the Shantak. "Mine is a piece of crap."

Larry unlocked the door, and Lake settled into the passenger seat, admiring the car's interior.

"It's nicer than I expected, sir," she commented.

"Thanks... I think," Larry responded with a hint of uncertainty.

"You're welcome, sir," Lake replied.

Larry started the car and pulled out of the parking lot, heading toward his home. Curiosity got the better of him, and he decided to ask a question.

"So, what do you know about me?" Larry inquired.

"Not much, sir. Only what Superintendent Gaunt told me," Lake admitted.

"And what did she tell you?" Larry pressed further.

"She said that you were a good man and that I should obey your every command as if it came from her," Lake revealed.

Larry pulled into his parking space, bringing the car to a stop.

"Welcome home, sir," Lake greeted him.

"Thank you... I suppose," Larry replied, still processing the unusual turn of events.

They exited the car and made their way up to the apartment, embarking on an unexpected evening together.

Chapter 16

"Is that your daughter?" Lake asked, gesturing toward Dani.

"Yep, that's Dani," Larry confirmed.

Lake complimented Dani, saying, "She's beautiful, sir."

"Thank you," Larry replied with a smile.

Dani was sitting on the couch, engrossed in a game on her phone. When Larry and Detective Lake entered, she glanced up and frowned.

"Hey, Dad," Dani greeted him.

"Hey there, sweetie!" Larry responded warmly.

He took a seat next to Dani and leaned in to give her a kiss on the forehead.

"How was your day?" Larry asked, showing interest in her activities.

"It was alright. How was work?" Dani inquired, reciprocating the curiosity.

"It was tough. This is Detective Lake. She's been assigned to my team to replace another officer who's in the hospital," Larry explained.

"This is Dani," he introduced his daughter to Detective Lake.

"It's a pleasure to meet you," Lake said politely, extending her hand. "You can call me Farley," she added, acknowledging the informal nature of their conversation.

Dani shook Lake's hand, offering a friendly response, "You too."

Lake settled on the couch beside Larry, her presence blending into the family dynamic.

"My data analyst, Detective Pabodie, found out she was pregnant today. So she's going to be on leave for a while. Farley here is taking her place," Larry informed Dani.

"That's great, Dad," Dani replied, though her attention remained focused on her phone.

"I'm going out to get some food. Want anything?" Larry asked, considering Dani's preferences.

"Yeah, a salad," Dani requested. "I'm trying to eat healthier."

"Since when?" Larry questioned, slightly surprised.

"Since now," Dani answered matter-of-factly.

Larry stood up and turned to Lake.

"You like sushi, Farley? There's a new place that just opened up down the street."

"I love sushi," Lake responded with enthusiasm. "Let's do it."

Larry looked at Dani, hopeful that she might have had a change of heart.

"What do you think, Dani? Sushi? It's healthy."

Dani scrunched her nose in dislike.

"I hate fish, Dad," she groaned. "Why do you keep asking me if you already know?"

"I thought maybe you had grown up since I asked last," Larry teased lightly.

"I'm 14, Dad. Not 4," Dani retorted, rolling her eyes.

"Fine, no sushi for you," Larry conceded, pretending to be defeated.

He walked toward the door but turned his head back to Dani, giving her a shrug.

"Be back in an hour."

With that, Larry stepped out, leaving Dani to her game.

¤

It was a short walk to the sushi restaurant, and Farley remained quiet as they strolled along. Larry pushed open the door and stepped into the establishment. Inside, they were greeted by the sight of a long wooden bar with stools, manned by an older man with a shaven head, a white chef's hat, and a bushy mustache. The man nodded at their arrival.

"Welcome!" he exclaimed, striking a small gong. "How many will there be?"

"Just two," Larry replied.

The man motioned for them to follow him and walked around the bar, leading them to a cozy booth in the corner of the room. He seated them and handed menus to both Farley and Larry.

"I'm Hiroshi, and I'll be your waiter this evening," he introduced himself. "Today's special is the tuna tataki, and our sushi of the day is Isaki. Can I get you drinks?"

Larry glanced up at Hiroshi and nodded. "I'll have a diet soda."

Farley chimed in, "I'll have the same, please."

Hiroshi smiled and made his way back to the bar to fetch their drinks.

As Larry looked across the table at Farley, he noticed her genuine smile. The waiter returned with their drinks, and they placed their order, engaging in casual conversation as they awaited their food. The atmosphere was relaxed, and their interaction flowed effortlessly. Larry found himself enjoying Farley's company more than he had expected.

The waiter returned once again, this time placing a small bowl of edamame on the table. Larry expressed his gratitude, taking out a pod and popping it into his mouth. Farley followed suit, and they continued their conversation. A few minutes later, the waiter returned with their food. They both indulged heartily, savoring the flavors, and soon their plates were empty.

"So, Farley," Larry began, wiping his mouth with a napkin. "Did you specifically choose to work with me?"

Farley paused for a moment, contemplating her response. "Yes, it was my first choice. I actually applied to a few different departments, but I found homicide the most appealing. I wanted to work with you because I respect your methods."

Larry nodded, taking in her words. There was a sense of satisfaction in knowing that his approach had garnered respect from his new partner.

"Interesting," Larry remarked, a hint of intrigue in his voice.

Farley smiled, her eyes lighting up as she took a deep breath. "Are you finished eating?" she inquired.

"Yeah, I am," Larry confirmed.

"Then let's go," Farley said with a determined tone.

Larry settled the bill and led Farley out of the restaurant. They strolled back to his apartment building, noticing that the lights inside were turned off. Dani had already gone to bed.

¤

They entered the apartment and Larry found a note on the kitchen table.

'Don't think that I don't know what you're up to. -Dani'.

Larry crumpled the note and threw it in the trash.

"Your daughter is suspicious of you," Farley said.

"I'm well aware. What should we do about it?"

"Nothing. For now, at least."

Larry led her into his bedroom and locked the door.

Farley took off her overcoat and Larry realized that she was actually naked. The black dress was painted on her skin. He swallowed dryly and looked her up and down.

"See something you like?" Farley asked, running her fingers through his hair.

"You know I do. Come over here."

He sat on the bed and pulled her into his lap. She wrapped her legs around his waist and kissed him, forcing her tongue into his mouth.

Larry laid her down on the bed.

"Is there anything I need to know about you?" he asked.

"I'm allergic to bees. Otherwise, I'm perfectly healthy," she said.

Larry smiled and spread her legs. She was warm and wet just thinking about what he would do to her.

"I'd say I was surprised by your eagerness, but...."

"I want to be good for my boss."

Larry leaned in and kissed her passionately.

"Don't keep me waiting," she whispered in his ear.

"With pleasure," he replied.

¤

"What do we do now?" she asked.

"What do you mean?"

"Well... now what happens?"

"Nothing. We just lay here and... recuperate."

"OK..."

Farley turned to face him.

"What about Dani?" she asked.

"What about her? We're not doing anything wrong. We're not killing anyone, either."

"I know, but... I don't want to be the other woman. Dani's your daughter."

"Her mother was taken by the Overlords eight years ago. I haven't been with anyone in all that time."

Farley shrugged and turned away from him.

"I don't want to get in the middle of a complicated family drama," she said.

"Too late. Your handcuffed to my bed."

"Ha ha. You're funny. Let me up."

He put his arms around her and held her tighter.

"I'm just not sure about how Dani will take it. We've only just met and she's already giving me dirty looks."

"She'll be fine with it. I'll talk to her."

"Would you?"

"Sure. I can be a real charmer when I want to be."

"Great," Farley said.

Larry kissed her on the forehead.

"I'll go talk to Dani right now. You stay here," he said, checking the handcuffs and cupping a breast.

"I'll try, but I can't make any promises." He laughed as he put on a robe and headed out the bedroom door. He went to the kitchen where he found Dani.

"Hey Dani."

"Hey Dad," she replied, not looking at him.

"Listen, I need to talk to you about something."

"What?"

"Your mom's been gone a long time."

"I know that. I was just a kid when it happened."

"Yes, but... you don't miss her at all? Not even a little bit?"

Dani shrugged her shoulders.

"Everyone misses someone whenever they think about them," she said. "It's only natural, but some people grow out of it. Why? Do you miss her?"

"Of course I do," Larry said emphatically. "I loved her!"

"Yeah, but do you miss her? Like, do you feel a loss?"

"I do," Larry said, "but after all this time, I need to continue with my life."

"Then do it. Just let her go. I know you think by having someone new around, you'll eventually forget about mom. That's not how it works. Take it from me."

"I will never forget your mother! And Farley would never replace her. She's just a friend."

"Whatever you say, Dad."

"Dani, I just want you to be accepting of Farley. That's all I ask."

"Fine, I can do that."

He pulled her in for a hug and kissed her on the forehead.

"Thanks, baby girl. I love you."

"I love you, too, Dad."

"Now go to sleep. You have the Schola tomorrow."

"Good night."

Larry went back to the bedroom.

"Well, it sounds like you handled it," she said.

"I've had a lot of practice. Now, are you going to stay the night?"

"Is that an order, sir?

"I hardly know you!"

He climbed back into bed and wrapped his arms around her.

"In the future, Detective, I expect you to wear more appropriate attire!"

Chapter 17

In the morning, Larry dropped Farley off at her home before heading to the office. Dani preferred taking the bus to the Schola, so he respected her independence. As he arrived at the office, he found Horace already waiting for him, wearing a somber expression.

"Hey boss," Horace greeted him.

"Hello, Horace," Larry replied.

The reason for Horace's mood became apparent soon after.

"I'm sorry, sir, but we're out of coffee," Horace informed him.

"Out of coffee?!" Larry exclaimed.

"Yes, sir. The delivery never came."

"Send someone to Mother Hydra's! I need a jolt this morning."

"I'll go, sir," Horace volunteered.

"Thanks."

Larry made his way to his office and started sorting through the various papers on his desk. After a few minutes, he heard a knock on the door.

"Come in," he called out.

Horace entered, carrying two cups of coffee. He handed one to Larry.

"You are a lifesaver, Sergeant!" Larry exclaimed, taking a grateful sip.

"I aim to please, sir," Horace replied with a grin.

Larry shifted his attention to the ongoing investigation.

"Did they find anything at The Facility? Any records of the clones or the buyers?" Larry inquired.

"No, sir. There wasn't much left after the fire. They're still sifting through the rubble, but I don't know what they hope to find."

"What fire?" Larry asked, puzzled.

"The one that destroyed the place, sir. After we raided it, of course."

Larry frowned and took another sip of coffee, contemplating the situation.

"Where's the arson investigator? I want to discuss this fire with him," Larry questioned.

"Captain Isinwyll was killed last night, sir," Horace revealed.

"Killed? How?" Larry asked, his concern growing.

"It seems a thief broke into his home. He was found in his bed, stabbed through the neck."

"That's unfortunate. See if they can get any prints and track down this thief. It appears someone is tying up loose ends. Have we interrogated Dr. Llanfer or his staff yet?" Larry instructed.

"No, sir. They're still waiting in the interrogation room," Horace responded.

"Good. I'll head down there now and see what they have to say," Larry stated, preparing to leave.

Before he could step out, there was another knock on the door.

"Come in," Larry called out again.

Farley Lake entered, wearing her dress uniform, looking anxious.

"You wanted to see me, sir?" Farley asked.

"Yes. Sergeant Horace Whately, this is Detective Farley Lake. She'll be taking Gwen's place as our data analyst," Larry introduced them.

"Hello," Horace greeted, shaking Farley's hand.

"Pleasure to meet you," Farley replied.

"Is Alan in yet, Horace?" Larry inquired.

"No, sir. Do you need him for something?" Horace asked.

"No, I just figured he'd be in by now. Send him in here as soon as he arrives. That will be all," Larry instructed, dismissing Horace.

Farley took a seat as Larry watched her, appreciating her attractive appearance and confident demeanor.

"The uniform is a nice touch, but is that a regulation skirt?" Larry teased.

"Yes, sir, it is," Farley replied, maintaining her composure.

"Do you have a problem with it, sir?" Farley responded, meeting his gaze.

"Not at all," Larry replied with a smirk. "Tell me, Farley, do you like your new job?"

"I love my job, sir," Farley answered.

"You love it? Why?" Larry probed further.

"I enjoy working with the technology, sir. I like being on the cutting edge of information," Farley explained.

"And?" Larry pressed on.

"And... I also enjoy the field work, sir. I won't deny it," Farley admitted, a hint of a smile playing on her lips.

"Good. Now go find Lisa Taylor," Larry instructed.

"Yes, sir. Right away, sir," Farley responded promptly, getting up from her seat.

As Farley left the office, Larry found himself alone, surrounded by the papers and files demanding his attention. However, he realized that he hadn't eaten anything yet that day. The diner across the street beckoned to him, promising a much-needed meal.

Setting aside his work momentarily, Larry took a break and satisfy his hunger.

¤

The diner was relatively quiet at that early hour of the morning. Larry took his usual seat at the back, enjoying the rich aroma of his coffee. He didn't plan on staying long, intending to savor his cup before returning to the Police Presidium.

As he was about to leave, a voice called out his name. Larry turned to see Superintendent Gaunt approaching him. Her expression was one of fury, and she appeared visibly agitated.

"What can I do for you, Superintendent?" Larry inquired, trying to maintain a calm demeanor.

"Tell me everything about the Crouchman case!" she commanded.

Larry complied, recounting the events that led him to the Crouchman mansion and the discoveries he made inside. When he finished, Gaunt raised an eyebrow, clearly displeased.

"Crouchman has connections to everything in this city, especially half of the top brass," Gaunt sighed, the weight of the situation evident in her voice.

"It seems that the old sword was used to kill the Overlord. It was found near the body, and Crouchman appeared to have been mauled to death, presumably by the Overlord," Larry explained.

"There was an investigation into that sword three years ago. It shouldn't even exist. A weapon like that..." Gaunt trailed off.

"Shouldn't exist? What do you mean? What makes it so special?" Larry inquired, sensing Gaunt's hesitation.

Gaunt stared at him, her eyes betraying a hint of fear. "The only ones capable of crafting that sword are long dead. If they're not dead, they're in their metaphorical graves. The art of creating such weapons died out centuries ago."

"How does this connect to the dead Overlord?" Larry pressed for answers.

"How do you think a regular human, or any mortal, managed to bring down an Overlord?" Gaunt asked, her tone flat.

"The sword?" Larry speculated.

"Yes, the sword. It serves a specific purpose: to kill Overlords. That's why it was created. It's a rare and forgotten craft, but it's not the only one. There are other weapons out there—special, powerful weapons—all designed to eliminate the Overlords," Gaunt explained, her words filled with a mix of knowledge and intrigue.

"But the Overlords only arrived one hundred years ago," Larry remarked, struggling to process the revelation.

"They didn't just arrive. They returned. How do you think I exist, otherwise?" Gaunt stated matter-of-factly. "The Overlords didn't simply appear out of thin air. They were here, once, long ago. And then they departed or ceased their visits."

"Returning to the matter at hand, how do you suggest we handle the higher-ups?" Larry redirected the conversation.

"Tell them the truth. A dead Overlord found in the home of a known crime lord is significant news. It will grant us more resources, more flexibility, and more of everything," Gaunt said.

"Crouchman was a crime lord?" Larry inquired, surprised.

"Crouchman was a pawn. He knew nothing. He's dead now. All we have to do is ensure the right people know the truth, and everything will be fine," Gaunt assured him.

Larry nodded, understanding the plan. "What do you want me to do?"

"Nothing out of the ordinary. Just continue doing your job. That's all," Gaunt concluded before leaving the diner. Larry decided to take a moment to have breakfast of bacon and eggs before returning to the squad room.

¤

"Horace, it's time to interview Dr. Llanfer," Larry announced as he entered the room.

"Finally? I thought we'd never get to it," Horace replied.

"You mean you've prepared?" Larry inquired.

"Yes, sir. I've been thinking about what questions to ask. Sir, are you okay?" Horace noticed Larry's distracted demeanor.

"What? Oh, yes. I'm fine," Larry responded, trying to shake off his preoccupation.

They proceeded to the interrogation room where Dr. Llanfer was restrained to the table, awaiting their arrival. He looked at Larry expectantly.

"Hello, Inspector. You're looking well," Dr. Llanfer greeted him.

"Hello, Dr. Llanfer. I'm here to ask you a few questions," Larry began.

"Go right ahead," Dr. Llanfer responded.

Larry started with a straightforward question, "How do you know Mr. Crouchman?"

"He was a patient of mine," Dr. Llanfer replied.

"For how long was he your patient?" Larry probed further.

"I fail to see why that's any of your concern," Dr. Llanfer retorted defensively.

"He's dead now, so confidentiality no longer applies," Larry reminded him.

"Alright, fine. He came to me three years ago complaining of severe chest pains," Dr. Llanfer reluctantly revealed.

"Go on," Larry encouraged him.

"That's it. I took care of him for about a year, and then I never saw him again until the night I was arrested," Dr. Llanfer explained.

"Where did you see Crouchman? At his house?" Larry inquired.

"Yes, at his house," Dr. Llanfer confirmed.

"Was anyone else present?" Larry pressed.

"His wife and son, possibly his daughter. I can't remember for sure," Dr. Llanfer replied.

"Did anyone witness your arrival or departure from the house?" Larry asked.

"His wife saw me enter, but she didn't see me leave. I'm certain she assumed I would stay the night," Dr. Llanfer answered. "I had stayed over before after a late-night house call."

Larry shifted the direction of the questioning, revealing crucial information. "No, Dr. Llanfer, Crouchman was not killed by you, but by an Overlord. And a Sarnath Khopesh sword, the same weapon used to kill the Overlord found at Crouchman's house, was also used to kill four of your clones."

Dr. Llanfer seemed puzzled. "I don't understand what you're talking about."

Larry persisted, demanding the truth. "Try again. What was Crouchman planning to do with those clones?"

"That's none of your concern," Dr. Llanfer retorted.

"Everything about those clones is my concern now," Larry asserted. "Now tell me about them. How long have you been creating them?"

"About a year, maybe two," Dr. Llanfer reluctantly disclosed.

"What was your intention with these clones?" Larry pressed further.

"Nothing. I already told you. They were solely for medical purposes," Dr. Llanfer maintained.

"I see. Sergeant, I need to use the restroom. Please keep our guest company," Larry instructed Horace.

Larry exited the interrogation room and made his way to the bathroom. He looked at himself in the mirror, his face reflecting the toll the recent events had taken on him. The stress had left him pale and worn out. He splashed water on his face, trying to rejuvenate himself.

Returning to the interrogation room, Larry found Horace standing up while Dr. Llanfer sat with a broken nose and a cut above his eye.

"Is there anything else you wish to share, Dr. Llanfer?" Larry questioned, trying to elicit more information.

"No, I think we're done here," Dr. Llanfer replied calmly.

Larry sighed in frustration. "I asked you a question."

"There's nothing else to tell you. I have nothing to hide," Dr. Llanfer maintained his stance.

Larry glanced at Horace, finding no answers in his expression. Determined, Larry crouched before Dr. Llanfer and locked eyes with him.

"Are you sure there's nothing more you want to share with me?" Larry demanded.

"Unless you murdered Crouchman and burned down my building, I have nothing to tell you," Dr. Llanfer taunted.

Larry lost his composure and grabbed Dr. Llanfer by the collar, forcefully slamming him into the table. "You're in no position to make jokes. What was the involvement of the Overlords in your research?"

Dr. Llanfer smirked back at him, his defiance evident. "I don't think you want to know."

"Try me!" Larry challenged him.

"Fine, if you really want to know, the Overlords provided funding for my research. They were interested in medical advancements, and saw the the potential in my work," Dr. Llanfer revealed.

"What potential?" Larry inquired, digging deeper.

"I was working on curing genetic diseases," Dr. Llanfer explained.

"That's it?" Larry pressed further.

"That's it," Dr. Llanfer affirmed.

"But the clones..."

Interrupting him, Dr. Llanfer clarified, "I already told you, they were merely spare tissue samples. Someone must have spun tales to make you believe I was creating an army of soldiers to take over the city or something. Now, are you going to charge me with a crime, or should I call my lawyer?"

"You are being charged with impeding an investigation. You will be detained here until your arraignment," Larry declared firmly.

Dr. Llanfer seemed momentarily concerned about his burned-down building. "By the way, what happened to my research?"

"Your building burned to the ground last night? The fire Inspector concluded it was due to a gas leak," Larry informed him, "before he was also murdered."

Dr. Llanfer was shocked. "Oh dear. All my hard work."

"Don't play innocent with me, Llanfer!" Larry warned.

"I'm afraid I don't know what you mean, Inspector," Dr. Llanfer said casually.

Exiting the interrogation room with Horace, Larry contemplated their next move. "Now we interrogate his 'assistant,' Jennifer."

Chapter 18

Larry and Horace walked down the hall to another interrogation room. Larry opened the door to find Llanfer's assistant standing with her wrists chained to the ceiling. She wore a bright red dress, which was ripped and tattered.

She noticed the Inspector and greeted him with a string of curses.

"Shut the hell up!" Larry yelled, frustrated with her demeanor.

She stopped smiling and laughed instead. "Oh, you like that? I can do more, cowboy."

Larry stared at her in disgust. He opened his mouth to speak, but Horace spoke first.

"What the hell happened to you?" Horace asked, concerned.

"I had a little run-in with these two gentlemen before you came in," she replied, gesturing towards the guards.

"She was being uncooperative, so we restrained her," one guard explained.

Larry motioned to the cameras in the room. "Turn them off."

"Why?" the guard questioned.

"Do you really need a reason? Turn them off," Larry commanded.

The guard complied, and the lights on the cameras went out. Jennifer looked puzzled.

"What the hell are you doing?" Jennifer asked.

"Shut up. Horace, grab her," Larry ordered.

Horace approached Jennifer and held her still. She struggled against his grip.

"Hey! Get off of me, you... ugh!" Jennifer exclaimed before Larry forcefully grabbed her chin, making her look at him.

"We know Llanfer isn't the brains of the operation. He just makes the clones. Since you were always at his side, I believe you are responsible for the business side of things," Larry stated firmly.

Jennifer laughed in response.

"Why the hell is she laughing?" Larry turned to Horace.

"I don't know, sir," Horace replied sarcastically.

Larry changed his approach. "Let me explain something to you. You are part of a conspiracy to defraud the Overlords and to commit murder. You are implicated in the deaths of four clones and Richard Crouchman. Your life as it was is over. If you cooperate, what comes next might be more bearable."

"A lot of good that'll do you. I don't know anything about Llanfer's business or whatever it is you think he's doing. I was his assistant, not his bodyguard or spy," Jennifer retorted confidently.

Larry's frustration grew, and he slapped her across the face. "Try again!"

Jennifer sniveled, "Yes."

"Good. Why don't you start by telling me what happened to Crouchman?" Larry demanded.

"I don't know much. He was acting strange for a long time. Refusing to meet with his contacts, even me. He wouldn't even meet with Llanfer at first. When he finally did, it was to tell him that things needed to change, or he'd turn him in. He kept going on about how the city was in danger and some other nonsense," Jennifer revealed.

Larry urged her to continue. "Go on."

"That's it, I swear! He wasn't making much sense, to be honest. He sent me to meet with Llanfer a few more times, but it was always the same thing. He wanted a cut of the profits, or he'd turn us in," Jennifer explained.

"And?" Larry pressed for more.

"I don't know. That's what I told him. That there was no way Llanfer would share his profits, and he knew that. There was no reason to threaten us," Jennifer added.

Larry continued his questioning. "How much money are we talking about, Jennifer? From Llanfer's ventures. You were his confidant. You must've had some idea of how much he was profiting from his business."

"I don't know the exact amount. He never let me see the books," Jennifer replied.

Larry's curiosity peaked. "Nothing at all? A guess then. A wild estimate?"

Jennifer hesitated before answering, "Well... he paid off half the officials in this town. Maybe two million credits a year?"

"Two million? You must be joking," Larry remarked, surprised by the figure.

"Do I sound like I'm joking? Two million credits. Every year. That's just the money that goes to the top officials," Jennifer clarified.

Larry took a moment to absorb the information. "I see. I guess we'll never know now. The Facility burned to the ground last night."

"And Crouchman?" Jennifer inquired anxiously.

"He was murdered in his home... along with an Overlord," Larry revealed.

Jennifer's face turned pale. "What? I... I had nothing to do with that, I swear!"

"I don't care. That's all I needed to know," Larry stated coldly.

He picked up her file and reviewed it once more before leaving the room. Larry made his way back up to the surface, stepping outside into the sunshine. The beauty of the day contrasted sharply with the darkness of his investigation. He knew it would be a long time before he could enjoy such a day again.

Larry phoned Horace to update him on the situation. "I've established that Crouchman and the Overlord are not connected to our clone killer. They killed each other. And neither of them killed the clones."

"I see. Anything else, sir?" Horace inquired.

"That's it, thank you," Larry replied with a sigh, feeling the weight of the case bearing down on him.

He leaned against the wall, deep in thought, contemplating his next move.

¤

After a few minutes of deep breathing, Larry returned to the squad room. He could tell from Farley's expression that she had something important to share.

"Well?" Larry asked eagerly.

"We found Jennifer Taylor's car abandoned. There was a significant amount of blood in the backseat," Farley reported.

"Is the blood hers?" Larry inquired.

"We're not sure. The DNA test was inconclusive. However, all of her personal belongings were still in the car, so it doesn't seem like she left willingly with someone else," Farley explained.

Larry's mind raced with possibilities. He needed more information. "Where is Officer Taylor currently assigned? Patrol? Which district?"

"Um..." Farley consulted her notepad, "Nir."

Larry's frustration grew. "Of course it is."

Just then, another officer approached them. "Sir, the CoCID wants to see you. It's something important."

Larry quickly headed to the CoCID's office. He knocked on the door, and the Superintendent's voice instructed him to come in. As he entered, he noticed that the office was crowded with officers, and Superintendent Gaunt stood at her desk, engaged in a heated conversation on the view screen.

"Superintendent," Larry greeted her.

Gaunt waved him off, still engrossed in the conversation. The other officers in the room glanced at Larry, some nodding in recognition, while others looked tired and worn out. Among them, Larry spotted Captain Hayes, who winked at him and mouthed the words, "Good luck."

They all heard a deep accented voice emanating from the view screen. "Gaunt, I don't care if your men are tired. They agreed to the conditions of service when they signed up. If they aren't up to the task, then I'll send in..."

Gaunt cleared her throat, cutting off the voice mid-sentence. "I'm sorry, but I don't think my officers can continue tonight. We've been working tirelessly on this investigation."

"Very well, but I expect some progress by morning. You are dismissed," the voice on the screen replied sternly.

As the view screen went dark, Gaunt sat down and motioned for Larry to take a seat. He observed that Hayes and Farley were already seated together in the back of the room.

"I've just had an intervention from my boss, the Commissioner of Police. He's given me a deadline. By the end of the week, he wants results, or I'll be replaced, and you'll be taking over," Gaunt informed Larry.

"What?! Me? I don't have the bloodline to hold your post!" Larry exclaimed, taken aback by the proposition.

"Maybe not, but I'll train you. It's time the humans had a voice anyway. Now, if you'll excuse me, I'm going home."

With that, Gaunt stood up and left the room. Larry turned to Hayes, seeking an explanation for the situation.

"What the hell is going on?" Larry asked, bewildered.

Hayes smirked. "Welcome to the club, boss."

Larry, speechless, turned away without uttering a word and left the room. He headed straight to his car and drove home.

¤

Sitting in the driveway, Larry stared at the building before him. The night enveloped him with its darkness, coldness, and solitude. The gentle wind seemed to nip at his skin.

He sat there, contemplating the weight and implications of becoming Gaunt's replacement. Holding a position at her level required having Overlord lineage, something Larry had never even considered. The thought sent shivers down his spine.

Finally, he gathered himself, got out of the car, and entered his apartment. Larry hung his jacket on a peg and was greeted by his daughter Dani.

"Hey, Dad!" she cheerfully greeted him.

"Hey, honey," Larry responded, his voice devoid of emotion.

"What's wrong?" Dani asked, concerned.

"Work stuff," Larry replied, walking into the living room and collapsing onto the couch.

Dani followed him, her caring nature evident. "Is it that bad?"

"You could say that," Larry sighed.

"Well, maybe it'll get better," Dani offered, trying to provide some comfort.

Larry managed a smile, grateful for his daughter's optimism. He embraced her tightly and said good night.

"Good night, Dad," Dani whispered before leaving him to his thoughts.

Larry retreated to his bedroom, falling onto the bed and shutting his eyes. Exhausted, he succumbed to sleep, his mind filled with uncertainty and anticipation for the challenges that lay ahead.

¤

Larry sat in the CoCID's office, his mind filled with confusion. Farley knelt beside him, but something seemed off. She was wearing a black leather collar and a leather corset, an unusual sight for the squad room. Larry's discomfort grew as he took hold of Farley's leash and led her through the squad room.

To his surprise, all the officers wore black, form-fitting coveralls and face-shielding helmets. The only contrasting feature was the badge-shaped insignia. As he passed, they pressed their right fists to their chests and saluted by raising their fists.

Unsettled, Larry took Farley with him into the elevator, heading up to the fiftieth floor. Stepping out, they entered a long hallway lined with offices. Each office had a door facing the hallway, equipped with a square, 2D video screen displaying various faces—male, female, human, alien. Although different, they all seemed eerily similar.

Approaching the office at the end, Larry opened the door and was greeted by a massive room. The ceiling towered several stories high, and a grand mahogany desk dominated the center. A golden nameplate on the desk read: LAZARUS NODENS, COMMISSIONER.

Larry took a seat behind the desk, with Farley standing beside him. Pressing a button, he called out, "Lieutenant Lake."

"Yes, sir? How may I help you?" the voice inquired.

"I'd like a cup of coffee and a chocolate sundae," Larry requested.

"Certainly, sir. Anything else?" the voice responded.

"That will be all."

As the walls of the room transformed into high-definition screens, displaying various locations within the Police Presidium, Larry watched for a while before deciding to get his coffee and sundae. He sat back down, indulging in his treat. Just two minutes later, there was a knock on the door.

"Come in," Larry called out.

The door opened, and to his surprise, a grown-up Dani entered the room. She was dressed in black pants, a black shirt, a dark red jacket, and black boots. Her features had matured, showcasing sharp angles and thin lips. Her blond, curly hair framed her face, while her small eyes gazed at Larry.

"It's time for your next treatment," Dani informed him, holding up a hypospray.

"Hold on. Let me finish this cup," Larry replied, taking a final gulp of his coffee.

Dani patiently waited, and as soon as Larry finished, he held out his arm. She injected him with the hypospray, and Larry took a deep breath, preparing for the familiar pain to fade away. But something went wrong. The pain intensified instead of dissipating, leaving Larry bewildered.

Opening his eyes, he noticed that his skin had taken on a bluish tint. His ears felt swollen, and his veins pulsed visibly, resembling rivers on a map. Everything around him seemed amplified—the hissing of the lights, the clinking of ice in the soda machine, the buzzing of the fluorescent lights. It was overwhelming—too loud, too bright, too big.

"Sir?" Dani's voice boomed, looking at him with concern.

In a sudden surge of instinctual panic, Larry stood up and lunged at Dani. He grabbed her with his four arms, and in an instant, they both disappeared.

¤

Larry woke up abruptly, his body drenched in sweat. The remnants of a vivid dream clung to his mind, leaving him disoriented. Dani stood by his bedside, her face troubled.

"You were tossing and turning, and you seemed distressed. Are you OK?" she asked, her voice filled with genuine worry.

Larry glanced around, gradually realizing that it was just a dream that had shaken him so intensely.

"I'm fine, honey. It was just a nightmare," he reassured her, attempting to calm his racing heart.

"Do you want to talk about it?" Dani inquired, her eyes filled with empathy.

"No, it's not important," Larry replied, wanting to dismiss the haunting images that still lingered in his mind.

Glancing at the alarm clock, he noticed that it was nearly midnight. Confusion mixed with relief as he realized that he had been caught in the grip of his imagination.

"Why are you still awake?" Larry asked, shifting his focus to Dani.

"I could ask you the same thing," she responded, a gentle smile gracing her lips.

"Go back to bed. I'm fine," he insisted, wanting to reassure her.

"I love you," Dani expressed, her voice filled with warmth and affection.

"I love you too," Larry replied, grateful for the comforting presence of his daughter.

With that, Dani bid him goodnight, leaving Larry to collect his thoughts and calm his racing mind. As he lay back in bed, he reflected on the power of dreams and the solace of love, hoping that the night would bring him a peaceful slumber.

Chapter 19

Larry awoke the next morning with resolute determination. After having breakfast and dropping Dani off at school, he made his way to the Police Presidium, heading straight for Superintendent Gaunt's office. He knocked on the door, awaiting permission to enter.

"Enter," Gaunt's voice called from within.

Larry stepped into the office and took a seat. Gaunt sat behind her desk, a composed expression on her face.

"I will not take your place as CoCID," Larry stated firmly, determined to make his position clear.

"I'm not asking you to," Gaunt responded calmly, her voice steady. "You will apprehend the clone murderer by the end of the week."

Confusion filled Larry's mind as he struggled to comprehend the gravity of the situation. He couldn't help but voice his bewilderment.

"What? Why? What is happening?" he questioned, seeking answers.

Gaunt's grin only deepened, and she responded cryptically, "I don't have to tell you anything. Now, get out of here. I have work to do."

Realizing that further discussion would be futile, Larry left Gaunt's office and made his way back to his own. To his surprise, he found a large envelope waiting for him on his desk. Curiosity piqued, he opened it and discovered a file. It contained information about the first victim of the killer, Susan Jones, the singer. Alongside the file was a note with a clear message:

You have three days. Use them wisely.

Determined to make the most of the limited time he had, Larry summoned Alan, Horace, and Farley into his office. As they gathered, he closed the door and addressed them, emphasizing the urgency of the situation.

"We must catch the killer within the next three days," Larry declared, his tone serious. "There are a lot of eyes on us, especially on me. If we fail to apprehend the killer by the end of the week, the consequences will be dire."

His team listened attentively, aware of the weight of the task at hand.

"We have identified four of the six clones, including the first victim, Susan Jones," Larry continued, referring to the file he had received. "Officer Taylor is still missing, and we need to locate her. Find out everything you can about her car and the blood found in it. We need immediate identification."

Alan nodded, acknowledging the importance of the task. "I'll put pressure on the lab to expedite the analysis."

Larry's gaze swept over his team, his resolve unwavering. "There are only two clones remaining: Karen Stone, the cook, and Heather Jensen, the doctor. We must find them and bring them in, preferably alive."

Horace and Farley exchanged determined glances, ready to take on the challenge.

Larry turned his attention to Farley, who was still by the door. "Farley, I need you to investigate if there have been any other deaths, suspicious or otherwise, involving individuals resembling our clones. If the perpetrator has targeted another lookalike, it may provide us with valuable leads."

Farley nodded, acknowledging her task, before leaving to carry out her assignment.

With his team briefed and assignments given, Larry knew that time was of the essence. He sat back in his chair, contemplating the complex web of the case before him, determined to unravel the mystery and bring the killer to justice.

¤

Larry spent the rest of the day engrossed in reading through the case files, desperately searching for any clues that could lead him to the identity of the killer. Frustratingly, they were faced with a complete lack of viable suspects. They had ruled out anyone from The Facility, as there was no evidence linking Crouchman to the crimes beyond his association with Llanfer. The other individuals considered as potential suspects were only loosely acquainted with one of the victims, none of them having direct connections to all four.

Despite his exhaustive review of the files, Larry could not pinpoint any obvious leads or discern a pattern. He meticulously combed through the information once more, attempting to create a timeline of events and establish who had the most interaction with the victims. While he discovered a few gaps in the victims' schedules, there was nothing that offered a straightforward answer.

Shortly before the end of the shift, Farley entered Larry's office, breaking his concentration. He closed a file and looked up, surprised to see her.

"Hey," she greeted him. "I wasn't aware you were still here."

"Just going over some case files," Larry replied, gesturing towards the piles of papers on his desk. "Anything new?"

Farley shook her head. "Not really. I just wanted to see you, but I know you're busy. I'll see you tomorrow. Good night, sir."

"Good night, Farley," Larry responded, watching as she left the office. Now alone, he stared at the stacks of papers before him, realizing that the killer remained at large. Determined to make progress, he picked up the file Farley had recently left on his desk, intrigued by its contents.

Examining the top paper, Larry deduced it to be a medical report, with "CN" scribbled on it by Dr. Llanfer, presumably indicating Claire Noble. Setting it aside, he glanced through the other papers without delving deep into their contents. Each file pertained to one of the six clones, and Larry was taken aback by the meticulous record-keeping by Llanfer.

As he reviewed the files for Heather Jensen and Alison Craven, they appeared fairly standard. However, when he reached Lisa Taylor's file, he noticed something peculiar. Comparing it to Karen Stone's file, Larry observed a stark difference. Karen's file contained extensive and detailed notes about her habits, thoughts, and feelings, far more elaborate than the others. It almost seemed like a personal diary rather than clinical documentation. The same held true when he examined Lisa's file.

Intrigued, Larry wondered if there was a deeper connection between Dr. Llanfer and Lisa Taylor. He pulled out Lisa's file and discovered a photo tucked behind the front cover. It wasn't a professional portrait but rather a candid snapshot, seemingly taken by a friend. Lisa wore a cap and smiled gently at the camera. However, when he turned the page, he was taken aback by what he found.

The same photo was clipped to the inside cover of the folder, accompanied by a small post-it note with the word "Lisa" scrawled in block letters. Surprised and intrigued, Larry turned the photo over to check the back but found nothing written. He carefully placed it down and repeated the process with Heather and Alison's files, examining the photos attached to their inside covers. Neither had anything written on the back.

Driven by curiosity and a growing sense that these details were significant, Larry skimmed through several pages of each file, shifting the pictures clipped inside. As he examined Heather's file, he made a startling discovery. Another note was clipped to the inside cover, stating, "Must save Alison." There was no question mark, only an assertive statement.

Puzzled, Larry pondered the meaning behind these discoveries. Collecting the files, he decided to take them with him to the interrogation room, hoping that a change of environment might provide some clarity.

¤

Larry called for Dr. Llanfer to be brought in and restrained, handcuffing him to the table in the interrogation room. He placed the files in front of the bewildered doctor, his tone demanding answers.

"What's the meaning of this?" Larry questioned, his gaze fixed on Llanfer.

Confused, Llanfer looked at the files, trying to comprehend the situation. "I don't understand," he replied, his voice filled with uncertainty.

"These are your files on Heather Jensen, Karen Stone, and Lisa Taylor—clones one, two, and three. But there are far more notes on Karen than on Lisa and Heather. Why is that?" Larry pressed, his eyes narrowing with suspicion.

Llanfer appeared flustered, attempting to deflect. "I don't know what you're talking about," he stammered.

Larry's patience wore thin as he confronted the doctor. "Talk to me, doctor. I need to catch the killer responsible for their deaths."

Reluctantly, Llanfer opened up. "I had a daughter once," he confessed softly, his gaze distant. "She would be about their age now."

Sympathy softened Larry's expression. "What happened to her?"

Llanfer's voice quivered with grief. "Car crash. She died at that age. A drunk driver hit her."

Expressing condolences, Larry said, "I'm sorry for your loss."

Llanfer's demeanor shifted, bitterness seeping into his voice. "I made a deal with the devil. Now I've lost everything."

Curiosity piqued, Larry pressed further. "What did he do to you?"

Imparting a cryptic response, Llanfer whispered, "Come on, detective, you already know. You saw the bodies."

Frustration mounting, Larry demanded clarity. "I don't understand what that means. You better start talking straight with me, Dr. Llanfer. I don't have time for games!"

Llanfer's tone turned philosophical as he spoke. "Death awaits us all. No one escapes it. Not even the great Dr. Llanfer."

Growing increasingly exasperated, Larry snapped, "So what did the Doctor sell his soul for? Immortality?"

A sense of longing colored Llanfer's words. "I wish. I wish I could turn back time, like that Crow fellow. I'd give anything to see my daughter alive again."

Seeking concrete answers, Larry pressed for details. "What did you do, exactly? Did you create the clones? What's the purpose of all this?"

Llanfer's response revealed a grander aim. "The purpose of all this? This was supposed to save lives. Hundreds of lives, maybe thousands. We could grow offerings for the Ravagers to prevent them from hunting down innocent people. Perhaps we could even find a way to prevent the random attacks altogether."

Absorbing the gravity of Llanfer's revelation, Larry probed deeper. "So the clones were created as an alternative to leaving corpses around the city at night. So what happened? Why aren't there any clones anymore?"

Llanfer admitted to the risks involved in their creation. "It was necessary to speed up the project. I took the plunge to see if it would work. And it did, but there was a risk of side effects."

"What kind of side effects?"

Llanfer's response was tinged with uncertainty. "We don't know. That's why we were closely monitoring Karen. Some of her physical attributes might have been heightened or lost altogether. Psychotic tendencies, violence. There is really no way of knowing without a proper autopsy."

Latching onto a crucial detail, Larry questioned Llanfer's favoritism. "So why is Karen your favorite? Why did you say you will miss her the most?"

A mix of emotions played across Llanfer's face before he admitted, "She was my favorite, detective. She's dead."

With a renewed sense of urgency, Larry challenged Llanfer, determined to uncover the truth. "So why was she your favorite? We haven't found her yet!"

Llanfer's voice trembled as he confessed, "She's my favorite because... because... I was the closest to her! I was the one who took care of her!"

Refusing to back down, Larry pushed further. "Who took care of the others? Give me the name of the person who tended to the other clones!"

Llanfer, feeling cornered, finally relented. "I did," he admitted, his voice tinged with defensiveness. "But I focused my attention on Karen. The others were looked after by my students."

Larry seized the opportunity, demanding names and addresses. "Your students? How many people worked on this project? Give me their names and addresses!"

Feeling defeated, Llanfer complied, entering the information for the six medical students into a tablet and passing it to Larry. The detective reviewed the details, noting that most of the students lived in Ivy Town, with a few in Old Dylath. With a plan forming in his mind, Larry contacted dispatch, instructing them to apprehend the students and bring them to the Police Presidium for questioning.

As the night wore on, Larry knew that he finally had some new leads that would propel the investigation forward.

¤

Larry swiftly grabbed his jacket and headed out the door, determined to find some answers. It was late, and the exhaustion was evident in his weary eyes. As he made his way towards his vehicle, a voice called out from behind.

"I'll see you in the morning, Sir," someone said.

Larry turned briefly, acknowledging the voice. "Yeah, I'll see you then," he replied before continuing on his way.

Driving home in his trusted Shantak, Larry's mind raced with thoughts of the case. He couldn't shake the weight of responsibility off his shoulders. Upon reaching his apartment, he entered to find Dani watching TV on the couch. Larry could sense her anticipation, waiting for him to share any leads he might have uncovered.

"So, any leads?"

Not wanting to burden his daughter or expose her to the gruesome details just yet, Larry deflected her question, concerned about her well-being. "So, have you had dinner, honey?" he asked, attempting to divert the conversation.

Dani's annoyance was palpable as she responded, feeling disregarded. "Yeah, I got dinner at the diner," she replied, her tone tinged with frustration at his avoidance.

Realizing his attempt to sidestep her question had fallen flat, Larry sighed, feeling the weight of his secrecy. "I honestly don't know much," he confessed, his voice heavy with weariness.

Dani's concern for her father overcame her irritation, and she spoke with sincerity. "Well... I'm here. If you need to talk, Dad..." Her words trailed off, offering a comforting presence.

Appreciating her understanding, Larry mustered a grateful smile. "Thanks, honey," he replied, touched by her support.

Both father and daughter retreated to their respective beds, seeking solace in the comfort of sleep. With a tired mind and a heavy heart, Larry closed his eyes, knowing that tomorrow would bring another arduous day. But for now, he found solace knowing that Dani was there for him, a pillar of strength in these troubling times.

Chapter 20

In the morning, Larry hastily had his breakfast and bid farewell to Dani before heading to his office. To his surprise, Superintendent Gaunt was already waiting for him, wearing a somber expression.

"Good morning, sir," Larry greeted him, noticing the frown on Gaunt's face.

"Morning, Inspector," Gaunt replied, his tone serious. "I'm not going to beat around the bush. We've got a serious problem. A serious PR problem."

Curiosity and concern filled Larry's mind as he leaned forward. "Sir?"

"The media, Inspector. They've discovered the existence of the clones," Gaunt revealed with a troubled sigh. "A few civil rights groups claimed that the clones were being held against their will. They obtained a court order, and when patrol executed the order, they found the bodies."

Larry's eyes widened in shock. "Whose bodies?" he asked, his voice laden with disbelief.

"Llanfer's students. Last night, the bodies of five medical students were discovered," Gaunt disclosed, his voice heavy with the weight of the tragedy.

"What? How did this happen?" Larry exclaimed, struggling to comprehend the horrifying turn of events.

"They're all dead, Inspector. But that's not all. Two additional bodies were found, a woman and a young girl," Gaunt continued, her words dripping with sorrow.

Larry's mind reeled at the magnitude of the tragedy. "Have they been identified?" he inquired, hoping for some answers.

"We don't know the identity of the woman yet, but the young girl has been identified as Molly Craven, the daughter of Alison Craven who was not a clone," Gaunt revealed, the severity of the situation sinking in.

Shock and grief washed over Larry as he grappled with the unfolding tragedy. "This is terrible. Are these new victims connected to our case?" he questioned, seeking some semblance of understanding amidst the chaos.

"I don't know, Inspector. But the public will expect answers, and they'll be looking to us for them," Gaunt stated, his voice filled with a sense of urgency.

Understanding the gravity of the situation, Larry composed himself, ready to take charge. "Understood, CoCID," he replied, a steely determination in his voice. Then, a realization struck him. "Wait! There were six students!"

Gaunt confirmed his suspicions. "The last student, Walter Stanczyk, is currently in hiding. He's considered extremely dangerous, and we need to find him, Inspector."

Realizing the significance of Walter Stanczyk's involvement, Larry's mind raced. "Walter Stanczyk is either our killer or has vital information about them," he concluded, his thoughts consumed by the urgency of the task at hand.

"You're familiar with him?" Gaunt questioned, surprised by Larry's knowledge.

"He was the one assigned to look after Dr. Heather Jensen," Larry informed, a mix of concern and determination in his voice.

Gaunt emphasized the importance of finding Walter. "Find him, Inspector. This is your top priority."

"Yes, CoCID," Larry replied, resolute in his determination to bring closure to the case.

Taking a moment to gather himself, Larry swiftly organized the investigation. He sent out an alert to all officers, instructing them to be on the lookout for the fugitive student. Soon after, he called his team into his office to provide them with the information.

"We're searching for one of Llanfer's medical students, Walter Stanczyk. Here's his file," Larry informed them, handing the folder to Horace.

Horace accepted the file and began reviewing its contents. "He was assigned as Dr. Heather Jensen's caretaker."

Alan chimed in with the information they had gathered so far. "We've checked her home and workplace. She hasn't been seen at either location since before we found the first victim."

Farley interjected, "Susan Jones was the first victim."

Alan acknowledged the correction. "Right, the first victim," he admitted.

Farley took charge of the situation, her sharp mind already analyzing the information. "Give me the file," she requested, and Horace handed it over. She quickly scanned through it, her mind racing with possibilities. "Sergeant, what are your thoughts?"

Horace pondered for a moment before expressing his opinion. "I believe this student has gone rogue. He could either be the killer or working in collaboration with them. We need to locate him fast."

"Considering he was responsible for Heather's well-being, we need to delve deeper into her life. Look into her friends, coworkers, habits, and hobbies. Let's gather as much information as we can," Larry instructed, his voice determined.

"Yes, sir," Farley acknowledged, ready to take on the task.

Larry turned his attention to another matter. "Have we located Lisa Taylor yet?" he inquired, hoping for some positive news amidst the grim circumstances.

Horace confirmed their progress. "She's currently in our holding cell, sir. She's visibly distressed."

With a heavy sigh, Larry contemplated the challenging road ahead. The investigation had taken a dark turn, and the weight of responsibility bore down on him. However, his resolve remained unwavering as he vowed to uncover the truth and bring justice to those affected by the unfolding tragedy.

¤

Larry descended to the holding cells, where Officer Taylor was being held. The officer on duty let him in, closing the door behind him. As he approached, he noticed her sitting on the bench, her head buried in her hands, tears streaming down her face.

"Officer Taylor?" Larry called out softly, trying to offer some comfort amidst her distress.

She looked up, her eyes red and puffy, and quickly stood, attempting to regain composure. "Yes, sir!" she replied, her voice shaky.

"At ease, Officer. Are you okay?" Larry asked with genuine concern, gesturing for her to sit back down.

She sat back down on the bench, nodding slightly. "Just... Need a moment, sir. It's been an incredibly stressful few days."

Larry sighed, understanding the weight of the situation. "I can only imagine. First, the killer, then the conspiracy, and now this."

Her head bobbed in agreement. "It feels like the whole world is turning against us, sir."

Larry took a moment to gather his thoughts before broaching a sensitive topic. "So, you're aware of your... counterparts," he said carefully, mindful of his choice of words.

She looked at him with a mixture of anger and sadness. "They're not my counterparts," she replied firmly. "I don't know what twisted family you've created here, but I want no part in it."

Larry immediately realized his mistake and offered an apology. "I'm sorry, Taylor. I chose my words poorly. But you know that you and the others are clones."

She looked away, her expression filled with a mix of pain and avoidance. "I don't want to talk about it," she murmured quietly.

"I understand that it's difficult, but it's important to address your feelings," Larry gently urged, hoping to help her process the overwhelming emotions.

She let out a bitter snort, clearly skeptical of the idea. "And what good will that do? Talking won't change the situation."

Larry maintained his calm demeanor. "We need to find the killer. Your safety is at stake as well."

She sighed, her guard momentarily lowering. "So, what do you want from me?"

Larry raised the folder he had brought with him. "We found evidence of a struggle in your car. Can you tell me what happened?"

She averted her gaze once again, her reluctance evident. "I don't want to talk about it."

Larry pressed on, emphasizing the urgency. "We need to find the killer. He has already murdered three of the clones. What if he targets you next? We must identify him."

"I told you, I don't want to talk about it!" she snapped, her voice growing louder before breaking into sobs once more.

Larry maintained his composure, his voice calm and reassuring. "I believe he attacked you in your car, but you fought back and managed to escape. Was the blood we found in your car his or yours?"

"It was his," she mumbled, her voice barely audible.

Larry's tone remained gentle as he continued his inquiry. "Do you know who the attacker was?"

She hesitated for a moment, her eyes filled with fear. "It was Stanczyk. Walter Stanczyk, one of Dr. Llanfer's students."

Larry's expression hardened, realizing the gravity of the situation. "Are you saying he attempted to frame you for the murders?"

Her voice quivered as she recounted her ordeal. "He... He was deranged. Kept saying we weren't human, that we needed to be eradicated."

Larry pressed for more details. "Can you recall anything else? Any mention of a conspiracy or other relevant information?"

"He mentioned a 'conspiracy' and said we were 'better off dead'," she replied, her voice trembling with fear and uncertainty.

"Thank you, Officer. Your information has been invaluable. We will take it from here," Larry assured her, acknowledging her bravery in coming forward.

She slowly stood up, her vulnerability evident. "When can I leave?" she asked, a glimmer of hope in her eyes.

"We need to process your release. It shouldn't take long since you are a cooperating witness and a victim. A tribunal will decide your fate, which may include reinstatement, demotion, or termination."

She shrugged, her expression resigned. "Whatever you decide, I guess. Just get me out of here."

"Of course. We're done here. An officer will escort you to see the psychiatrist for a mental assessment before your release," Larry informed her, his voice filled with compassion.

As Larry left the holding cells, he couldn't shake off the heaviness of the situation. The road ahead was fraught with challenges, and finding the truth seemed more crucial than ever.

¤

Larry returned to his office, deep in thought. On his way, he crossed paths with Farley.

"Farley, we have confirmation from Officer Taylor. It was indeed Stanczyk," Larry informed her, his voice laced with a mix of determination and concern. "He has expressed a belief that the clones should be eliminated. We need to act fast."

Farley nodded, understanding the gravity of the situation. "I'll disseminate his picture to all media outlets and make it clear that he is armed and dangerous. We should also send a team to his last known address."

Larry weighed the options carefully. "Put surveillance on his address for now. We don't want to spook him into hiding deeper. However, be prepared in case he decides to return there. We can't afford to let any chance slip through our fingers."

Farley raised a valid point. "He could have fled anywhere by now. It's a race against time."

Larry's expression grew determined. "Exactly. That's why we need to be vigilant and maintain a close watch. Let's hope our efforts pay off before anyone else finds him."

Farley straightened her posture, ready for the task at hand. "Yes, sir. I won't let you down."

With a final exchange of determined glances, Larry and Farley parted ways, each focused on their respective roles in the urgent hunt for Walter Stanczyk. The stakes were high, and the clock was ticking. The race to apprehend the dangerous fugitive had begun.

¤

Larry approached the office of Superintendent Gaunt and knocked on the door, waiting for permission to enter. Gaunt's voice beckoned him inside, and he stepped in to find her engrossed in her datapad, focused on the task at hand.

"Inspector Nodens, report," Gaunt said without looking up, her tone brimming with urgency.

Taking a composed stance, Larry provided the update. "We have positively identified the killer as Walter Stanczyk, a medical student. He poses an extreme danger."

Gaunt's brows furrowed as she absorbed the information. "A doctor? Why would he harbor such animosity towards the clones? What could be his motive?"

Larry relayed Officer Taylor's account. "According to Officer Taylor, Stanczyk was overheard expressing his belief that the clones are not human and must be eradicated. We are currently working to locate him. Our preliminary search indicates that he is not at his residence or the university. We have issued an all-points bulletin and anticipate apprehending him soon."

Gaunt nodded with a sense of urgency. "Excellent. The sooner we take him into custody, the better. The public's unrest is already reaching critical levels. We must find a way to quell their anger."

"Understood, CoCID. Rest assured, my team and I are committed to resolving this swiftly."

Gaunt dismissed him with a firm tone. "Dismissed, Inspector."

Larry turned and left Gaunt's office, his mind already racing with plans and strategies. As he returned to the squad room, he knew the task ahead was crucial. The clock was ticking, and the city's stability hung in the balance. Determined and focused, Larry prepared to rally his team, for the hunt for Walter Stanczyk had reached a critical phase.

¤

Upon his arrival, Larry noticed Farley engaged in conversation with another officer. The man, Commander Ward, exuded an air of authority and was clad in the tactical officer's uniform.

Farley acknowledged Larry's presence with a nod. "Inspector, this is Commander Ward. He's leading the Armed Response Squad."

Larry extended a polite greeting. "Pleasure to meet you, Commander."

Ward responded with a contemplative expression. "Quite the conundrum you have here, Inspector."

Curious, Larry inquired further. "What do you mean, Commander?"

Ward explained, his gaze fixed on Larry. "On one hand, you're dealing with a serial killer. On the other hand, the victims are not considered human beings."

Farley interjected, emphasizing the distinction. "They're clones, not actual people."

Acknowledging Farley's statement, Ward continued. "Yes, Farley, we're all aware of that. What I mean is that from a legal standpoint, it may not meet the criteria of terrorism. Superintendent Gaunt shares a similar view. She believes we should treat it as a crime and focus on finding the responsible individual."

Larry considered the implications. "Well, it seems the situation has gone beyond our control. The press has caught wind of the case."

Farley protested, asserting the importance of freedom of information. "You can censor the news."

Larry responded with a measured tone. "No, Detective, we cannot suppress information. However, we can exercise control over what and when it is reported."

Commander Ward sought clarification. "So, what would you like us to do, Inspector?"

Larry instructed him to stand by. "For now, Commander, remain ready. When there's a task at hand, we will inform you accordingly."

Ward accepted the directive with a nod and walked away.

Turning his attention to Farley, Larry sought an update. "Give me an overview of your inquiries. What's the current status?"

Farley provided insight into his investigations. "Heather Jensen has been operating in the city's underserved areas, primarily working at urgent care clinics. These clinics rely on manual record-keeping, making her harder to locate."

Understanding the situation, Larry concluded, "So, she's essentially in hiding."

Farley clarified, "In a way, yes. She's been practicing medicine discreetly, working at a clinic in Nir."

Larry made a decision. "Let's pay her a visit, Farley. It's time to gather more information directly from Dr. Jensen."

Chapter 21

Their journey to the clinic was a lengthy one, as Nir was on the northern outskirts of Dylath-Leen. The area was primarily an agricultural district, with automated farms and factories catering to the city's food production.

Upon their arrival at the clinic, Larry and Farley entered to find a burly man standing in front of the reception counter. With a shaved head, a prominent chin, and tattoos covering his arms, he exuded an imposing presence. Engaged in conversation with the nurse, he appeared agitated.

"I need to see the doctor, lady!" the man exclaimed, leaning over the counter. "I'm having trouble breathing."

"The doctor is currently with another patient," the nurse responded.

"Tell 'em it's urgent! I really need to see 'em," he insisted.

"I'll inform the doctor as soon as she finishes with her current patient," the nurse assured.

"This is serious! I can barely breathe!" the man persisted.

While they conversed, Larry surveyed the waiting room. Typically bustling with patients, it was unusually empty, with only the man present.

Approaching the nurse, Larry inquired, "What's your name?"

"Rita, why?" she responded, visibly annoyed by the interruption.

"I'm Inspector Nodens from CID, and this is Detective Lake. We need to speak with Dr. Jensen urgently," Larry explained, showing his credentials.

Rita sighed in exasperation. "Oh, for the love of... I'll go get her."

She disappeared through a set of double doors, leaving Larry and Farley to wait patiently.

However, minutes passed, and Rita had not returned.

"Something doesn't seem right," Farley remarked. "You!" she addressed the injured man, drawing her gun. "Leave immediately!"

Larry also drew his pistol and signaled Farley to open the door behind the counter. With Farley covering him, Larry swiftly entered the room.

Inside, they found an examination room, equipped with an autoclave, an examination table, and various medical instruments unfamiliar to Larry. However, it was empty, except for a door that was intermittently swinging open and closed.

"Damn, they must have escaped," Farley said bitterly. "Damn it."

Larry motioned for Farley to be quiet, listening intently. From one of the doors along the short hallway, he heard a muffled moan.

The two doors on the left led to restrooms, while the first door on the right led to a janitor closet. The second door, labeled "Supplies," caught their attention. However, the source of the moaning seemed to originate from the door at the end of the hallway.

Larry attempted to open the door but found it locked. He knocked on the door, prompting someone inside to fumble with the doorknob. Suddenly, the door swung open.

A nurse, her hands bound and gagged with medical tape, stumbled into Larry, causing him to fall. Quickly recovering, he removed the tape from her mouth.

"Oh my God, you're a cop!" the nurse exclaimed. "He's going to kill them!"

"Calm down, what's happening?" Larry asked.

"There's a man holding the doctor and a patient hostage. He threatened to kill them if I called the police," the nurse explained.

"Does he have any weapons?" Larry inquired.

"He has a knife. He said he would kill the doctor first, then the patient if I contacted the police," she replied.

"How many hostages are there?" Larry asked.

"Just the two. He let another patient go. He was only after these two," the nurse revealed.

"Get out of here!" Farley commanded, grasping the woman's arm and urging her towards the swinging doors. "Find a police officer or a phone!"

Larry approached the closed door cautiously, listening to the commotion inside.

"I'm a doctor now!" a female voice shouted. "I help people, Walter! Why are you doing this?"

"She's not a person," a gruff male voice retorted. "And neither are you! You shouldn't exist!"

A scream echoed from within the room.

"No!" the doctor screamed.

Larry kicked open the door to confront a large man holding a woman in a lab coat as a shield. Bound to a chair with medical tape sat an identical woman wearing an apron, with a stab wound on her neck.

Larry aimed his gun at the man. "Shoot me, and the clone dies," the man threatened.

"You were planning to kill her anyway, right, Walter?" Larry said calmly.

"Let me go. I can help you," the woman in the lab coat pleaded.

"Shut up!" Walter shouted, striking the doctor.

Farley appeared in the doorway, gun drawn.

"Lisa Taylor is safe. You didn't get her. Your work isn't done yet," Larry informed Walter.

"Shut up! Shut up!" Walter yelled, striking his hostage again.

The woman in the lab coat subtly nodded to Larry.

Should I shoot? Larry pondered. I need him alive. I need to expose this lunatic to the media and capture his delusions.

"You need to release the doctor, Walter," Larry insisted. "You're a medical student. Your purpose is to save lives."

"Human lives! She's not human!" Walter shouted.

"You're a medical student. You're training to become a doctor," Larry argued.

"She's just as human as you and I!" Farley interjected.

Walter redirected his anger towards Farley, striking the woman again.

Larry pulled the trigger twice.

The woman collapsed to the ground. Larry hurried over to her, with Farley close behind.

"Are you hurt?" Larry asked.

"No," she replied. "I'm unharmed. He didn't hurt me. He couldn't hurt me. Only love can hurt, and it has never hurt me."

Larry paused, bewildered. "What? What does that mean?"

"It means she's mentally unstable," Farley remarked, stepping between Larry and the doctor.

"No! No!" the doctor screamed, struggling against Farley's restraint.

"He was in love with me," Jensen revealed. "That's why he couldn't kill me. He was torn between his hatred for clones and his love for me."

"Why did he love you but hate the other clones?" Farley inquired.

"He was assigned to take care of Lisa Taylor. She was violent and difficult. Walter wasn't cut out for parenting, but he ended up with a moody teenager. They didn't get along. He resented her," Jensen explained.

"But I wasn't a girl. I was a woman," Lisa Taylor interjected.

"Hello, Lisa," Heather Jensen greeted her.

"Hello, Heather," Officer Taylor responded, appearing behind Farley.

"We received a report of shots fired, sir," Officer Taylor informed Larry.

"Thank you for your concern, officer. We're fine, but this room needs to be secured. No one enters or leaves until my team arrives," Larry instructed.

"Yes, sir," Officer Taylor acknowledged before closing the door, cutting off all visual and audio contact with the outside world.

In front of Larry were two identical women: one deceased and one traumatized but alive.

"I'm sorry," Jensen said. "Karen was the gentle one," she said, running her fingers through the dead woman's hair. "All the children were kind, but she was the sweetest. All she wanted was to bring happiness, and she succeeded. She made me happy. She loved to sing. She gave Susan a run for her money. But Karen wasn't as outgoing as Susan."

Jensen turned her attention to Larry. "Who are you?"

"I'm Inspector Nodens, and this is Detective Lake," Larry introduced.

"I'm sorry, I don't know you. But I'm grateful you came."

Chapter 22

"Congratulations, Inspector," Superintendent Gaunt said as Larry stood before her desk, having just concluded his investigation.

"Thank you, sir," Larry responded. "If it's all the same to you, I'd prefer to work on murder cases rather than go through this again."

"Perfectly understandable. I'll keep that in mind. So, the case is solved. What are your plans now?"

Larry pondered for a moment before replying, "I'm not sure, sir. I suppose I'll take some time off and spend it with my daughter."

Larry left the Criminal Investigations Division's office, feeling a sense of accomplishment. As he made his way back to his desk, he gathered his few belongings without saying farewell to anyone. He simply departed, the weight of the recent case lifting off his shoulders.

Walking through the streets of Dylath-Leen on his way home, Larry's mind buzzed with a whirlwind of thoughts. The faces of his colleagues, particularly Farley, flashed before him. He couldn't help but chuckle, a rare laugh escaping his lips, followed by a warm smile.

Upon arriving home, Larry found Dani waiting for him. He informed her that he would be taking a few days off, a genuine smile gracing his face. Dani's eyes lit up, pleased at the prospect of spending more time with her father. Though no words were exchanged, their connection spoke volumes.

Larry retreated to his bedroom, settling down on his bed. He contemplated how he should spend his newfound free time. Should he catch up on his reading, embark on a long-overdue home improvement project, or simply unwind and recharge? The possibilities were endless, and the excitement of having time for himself filled his thoughts.

As the evening wore on, fatigue embraced Larry, and he succumbed to the embrace of sleep. Pleasant dreams filled his mind, free from the weight of investigations and the demands of his profession. In that moment, he found solace and contentment, knowing that he had accomplished his duty and now had the opportunity to nurture his own well-being and cherish the time spent with his daughter, Dani.